Perilous Times

TJ Hemphill

TJ HEMPHILL ENTERTAINMENT
Southfield, MI 48075

TJ Hemphill also serves as a motivational speaker. To book Mr. Hemphill as a speaker, or to book any of his plays, please send your email to tjhemphillent10@gmail.com

ISBN: 1548802468
ISBN 978-1548802462
For Worldwide Distribution
Printed in the U.S.A.

Productions by TJ Hemphill

Lord, All Men Can't Be Dogs

God Don't Like No Ugly

Love Won't Let Me Wait

I'll Be Home for Christmas

Mama's Got a Plan

Taking Care of Business

Sapphire's Blues

Five Golden Rings

The Short Side of Life

Perilous Times

(All songs in the following story were written by TJ Hemphill with the exception of 'Oh Please Don't Let Them Crucify Him', written by Sharon Johnson)

In memory of

Willie and Leola Ervin

Ether France

Dedication

I dedicate this book to the memory and life of my dear mother, Doris Lee Hemphill-Cherry. The gift of her love is embodied in every spring as flowers that bloom, in every summer as the sun brings warm air, in every fall as colors diversify my thoughts, and in every winter as pure white crystals sparkling with joy.

From the Goodfellows Box (for those who know), to the small brown bag of goodies she provided every Christmas, her commitment and love to her children was as solid as the Rock she believed in.

Her tender sweet voice is heard in every song I've written and every note I've played. Her grace and her energy has been a tower of strength and hope to me, and I shall always be a better man because of her.

I also dedicate this book to the memory and life of Germaine Henrietta Hemphill, who gave me fifteen wonderful years of her life. My life with God seem to begin with her. I once said, "Lord let me love you the way she loved you." I will never forget you.

I dedicate this book to my brothers and sisters, Ola, Charles, Dolline, Ethel, and Derek. They were there with me at the beginning, in the Brewster Projects. We came out because God brought us out. Finally, to my children, LaRon, TJ, Paul, Amber, Mikal, Kadeem, and Jalen, who have always supported me no matter the circumstances.

Acknowledgements

No man can measure himself by himself. It is the beauty and talents of others that make any vision possible—from the hundreds of actors, especially William Murphy III, Jeff Mickens, and LJ Covile, to all the people behind the scenes of the stage production that inspired this novel.

To my sons and daughter, whom I love and whose support I will always cherish. To my pastor, Reverend Solomon Kinloch, a man of wisdom well beyond his years, who supported me when I needed him most, and whose vision for the advancement of young people in the Kingdom of God through the Triumph church family, is embodied in these pages and certainly lies in juxtaposition with the intent of this novel. To my friends, Dr. James and Loretta Morman, who were there for me during some very trying times. To Dr. Cullian Hill and Angela Moore, who afforded me the opportunity to teach hundreds of students at Commonwealth Community Development Academy in Detroit. To my late mentor and friend, Bishop Wilbert S. McKinley, who spent hours and hours late into the night teaching me the Word of God. To Kristina King, whose hard work and dedication to my success can never be measured. She was there when life seemed to end for me. To Kimberly Moore and Greg Dunmore, whose thoughtfulness and support continues to inspire me. To Lindsey Franklin, who is an editing genius. Her guidance was priceless. To Cathy Nedd, whose labor of love in the beginning of this project I could never afford.

To my Hemphill Entertainment team and very special friends, Shy Averett, Deborah Boatner, Kelly Stubbs, Shirley Smith, and Lakiya Neal, all of whom I love so dear, and especially to Elonda Moore, who always has my back, and who just may be an angel in disguise.

Finally, to every teenager, young person, man or woman, struggling to find his or her place in this world. You were the inspiration for me to write and produce the stage play, *Perilous Times*, which led to this book.

And finally, to He to whom I owe all things, to the lover of my soul, even Jesus Christ, I give all the glory for the things He has done, is doing, and shall do.

Foreword

It has always been my belief that in order for a man's proclivities, habits, or sentiments to change, there first must be a change in his spirit. The "soulish" man can never depend on his intellect or his natural talents to deliver him from a society on the brink of anarchy. One look in the Bible at the last chapter and last verse in the book of Judges can give you a very clear picture of where we are today. Even a person overflowing with all the wisdom of King Solomon, or a keen and perspicacious mind like President Barack Obama, cannot be shielded from the poisonous tendrils of current world socialism and capitalism.

This book, based on my stage production of the same title, represents a microscopic view into the world of an average young adult, specifically from an average urban city. What ails Detroit, ails all urban cities in America. The solution to these problems, in my humble opinion, rests in the pages ahead. It has proven to me to be the only real answer to the growing social epidemics that face our society and particularly our young people today.

Whether one enjoys this book purely as a narrative fictional delight, or whether one enjoys it as a door-opener to the wonderful world of Christianity, the hope is that a fresh awareness of the sacrifice of a man named Jesus, will provide a real solution—or at least an alternative—to the dead-end road of drugs and promiscuity, and the love of money.

"This know also, that in the last days, perilous times shall come."

2 Timothy 3:1 (KJV)

CONTENTS

There's a way of life that looks harmless

enough; look again...Proverbs 14:12

Chapter 1

Trouble at Home

Bobby's life flashed before his eyes. A siren and bullhorn blasted his eardrums, screaming from the police cruiser chasing him and his friends through the streets of Detroit's eastside.

Bobby gripped the center console as they raced up Forest Avenue, all the way up to Cadillac Street, and back down Warren Avenue. Their Dodge—brand-new, black, with shining rims—did its best to outrun the charged-up, blue police vehicle. But the cops were gaining ground. Fear gripped everyone inside the car, plain on their faces.

Everyone except Mike.

Mike's mouth stretched into a grin, the chase seeming to stoke the thrill-seeking fire that always smoldered just beneath Mike's surface. No surprise to Bobby. Mike thrived on these exploits in the city.

Bobby's gut twisted at the thought of his mother's anger if he landed in jail. Again. Mike laughed and the engine roared like he'd just floored it. Bobby glanced at the dashboard clock. Almost twenty minutes since the police had started chasing them. Over the screech of tires and the wail of the siren, a new sound joined the music of the pursuit. Bobby turned his eyes toward the sky and the chop-chop-chop of...

Helicopter blades. His heart sank.

The silver police helicopter hovered overhead, at times blending into the gray skies over the city.

A piercing voice cut through the chaos. "Pull over now!"

Mike swerved the car around the corner of East Grand Boulevard. "Aw, crap! I ain't going down like this! Not today." The car was nearly on two wheels as it skidded into an alley behind an old funeral home. One hand on the wheel, Mike swallowed the green contents of a small plastic bag. Though the alley flashed by in a blur, Bobby knew it all too well. He moved his merchandise there, among other places—the business that was just starting to bring him a taste of the good life. Mike slowed the car enough that the blurs outside the windows turned to houses. He barked out to the rest of them. "Move!"

Finally. Now's my chance to get out of this mess.

Bobby took a deep breath, reached for the door handle, then pulled. He tumbled from the Dodge. The thuds on the ground nearby, told him his friends had done the same.

But Bobby didn't pause to make sure. He took off through the alley as fast as his legs would carry him. He spared a glance at the sky. The expanse overhead darkened just enough so the boys would be difficult to see.

Good.

Bobby ran from yard to yard. Mike overtook him once, and Bobby caught a glimpse of his other friends, Jason, Trevon, Raphael, and Troy, out of the corner of his eye as he cleared a fence. Still together.

He hopped another fence. A rosebush that may as well have been barbed wire, scraped his flesh as he landed. He winced, but there was no time to stop. His heart hammered in his chest—from running and from the adrenaline the chase produced.

Was it possible they'd be able to shake the cops? Maybe, if the dogs would stop barking. Yard after yard housed one of the yapping things, mostly pit bulls. The frenzied barks gave away the boy's location like blips on a radar screen.

Mike hoisted his husky frame over another fence, then turned and shouted back to Bobby and the others. "Split up! They can't catch all of us!"

Bobby and the others obeyed without question. Mike was their leader—and with a mile-long record and that stone-cold stare of his, why wouldn't he be?

Bobby, with only 165 pounds and just the beginnings of street toughness to his credit, certainly wasn't one to argue. He doubled back in the direction of the funeral home. In spite of the rush of the chase, a memory came flooding back to him. When the funeral home had been in operation, he'd seen two men bringing in a dead body covered with a white sheet. The recollection sent a chill through him. A snapping bark yanked him from the memory. Bobby glanced over his shoulder to see an ugly white pit bull had joined the chase.

Great.

Bobby thundered through several backyards, looking for a place to hide. Which would be worse, he wondered: being bitten by that nasty pit bull or being caught by the cops? He hoped to avoid both. One more fence to jump, then maybe he could. He dug his sneakers into the ground and sprang up, up, toward the sky. Toward freedom. But halfway through his flight, a piercing pain tore through his leg. He clumsily stumbled and slammed to the ground, barely clearing the fence. He stared at the ugly gash down his leg. Had he been shot? Had the dog caught up to him? But one glance upward revealed the culprit. The sharp point of a rusty fence, a common sight in the 'hood.

Bobby's heart raced so fast, he worried it might stop. Just like his father's heart stopped. He tried to push the thought aside but now wasn't the time. But that moment was etched in his memory as if in stone.

The look on his mother's face when she told him Dad had died.

Bobby could hear his own voice, calling out to him from the memory. *I didn't get a chance to say goodbye.* He felt his mother's arms around him, but the anger that still lived inside him bubbled up anew. Why had God taken his father away?

He could hear the words the preacher had spoken at Pleasant Grove Missionary Baptist Church during the funeral. "To be absent in the body is to be present with the Lord."

But it didn't mean anything. It was just an empty, hollow echo ringing in his ears, even now.

The chop-chop-chop of the helicopter cut through that echoed memory. Bobby had to move. Now. He scrambled to his feet. When his injured leg hit the ground, he grunted, but he had to keep going—keep moving forward.

And then he heard the words he'd been dreading, spoken by a threatening voice. "Stop! I said stop!"

No. Not now.

Bobby pushed harder. One more fence and he could hide in a windowless garage or his old church. The church was only another hundred yards, or so. That place where his mother went religiously every Sunday. That place where he last saw his father's face.

That place where he'd become so angry with God.

19

*I remember when the times when I first met the
Lord
I remember when the times when I had so much
peace and joy
I remember when I sang in the choir
How the Holy Spirit inspired
All the saints to sing with the fire
Lord I remember when
But now it seems like a different day
And the world seems so cold
I gave of myself day after day
But I got no return so I went on my way
And where were You when I needed You most
Someone to love me someone to care
But I remember yesterday
I remember but it seems so far away
I remember when*

He dashed toward his last hurdle. A warm
trickle of liquid told him his leg was bleeding pretty
good, but he ignored it. He sprang over the fence with
just enough room to spare. He tumbled onto the wet
grass, panting. The red-brick church loomed before him
like a challenge. He rejected this same church every
New Year's Eve and every Easter when his mother
dragged him there, but now he needed it. Music wafted
from the building—the same choir his mother begged

him to join, lifting their voices in adulation. Singing was the one thing Bobby did well. Just like Dad.

His mother's words rang in his ears so loudly; she may as well have been standing there with him. "Now boy, you know you should be singing in the choir. God will take that gift away from you and give it to somebody else if you don't use it."

He tried to tune out her remembered voice, he could hear her complaints about his clothes—the baggy pants, the plaid underwear, the hat cocked to the side, and the tattoos around his arms and neck that she hated so much. He shook his head as if he could shake his mother's disapproval from his mind.

Focus, Bobby!

That cop had to be close now. The sound of the choir reached a fevered pitch. The lead singer belted the words: "Jesus is the light of the world…"

Bobby had no choice. He had to get into the church. He brushed at the bugs crawling onto his Air Force 1s. He frowned, but he couldn't worry about the dirt on his sneakers, once pure white. Though dirty Air Force 1s were practically a sin in his crew, he didn't suppose the church folks would care. Every hurried step he took toward the church brought back the words of his old pastor. "God is my refuge and help in trouble."

Refuge. He'd never been able to understand it before, but now it certainly made sense. The church would be a place of safety where his enemies couldn't get to him. Somewhere he could find shelter.

Somewhere he could get away from trouble. Maybe he could sneak into the choir and blend in. He figured the police wouldn't be able to pick him out of there. They hadn't gotten a good look at his face. Maybe his old friends wouldn't snitch on him. Maybe the pastor would tell the cops he'd been here at the church the whole time. Maybe.

Bobby rubbed his wrists, raw from the steel handcuffs that had been clamped on before the police escorted him from the church. His heavily bandaged leg seemed to holler at him: "Crime doesn't pay!"

Stealing those jerseys from the mall had been a stupid idea, no matter what Mike said. Especially since they had enough money to buy them.

Robert, Bobby's out-of-touch so-called stepfather, stared straight ahead as he drove Bobby home. But first he had to make a quick stop downtown to handle some business. Robert hadn't said anything since he picked Bobby up from the police station, but Bobby knew that would only last so long.

As they rode through downtown Detroit, Bobby gazed out his window. It was almost as if he'd never seen the city until now. The majestic Fox Theater with its beautiful golden interior, and the Renaissance Center, which dwarfed every other building and was now General Motors headquarters, was just getting things started in Detroit.

Then there was Comerica Park, home of the Detroit Tigers. And Ford Field, where the Lions played football. Detroit hadn't won a football championship since1957 and had never played in a Super Bowl. Lastly, there was Little Caesars Arena, the new home of the Detroit Pistons and the Detroit Red Wings. Neither had championship-caliber teams. The brand-new arena glittered even though darkness had not set in.

The old-schoolers called Detroit the Motor City, but for Bobby, it was just home. Eminem, Trick Trick, Big Sean, and other hip-hop stars had long ago replaced The Supremes and The Temptations as the idols of youth culture. It had been years since Motown headed for the sunny skies and glamour of California. But who cared? Bobby and his crew were the generation of today. This was their city.

Bobby wanted everything that glittered and anything that shined like the sun, as long as it impressed his friends. And in the 'D', he could push his merchandise easily. Especially on the eastside. That place looked like a war zone. It never recovered from the 1967 riots, according to Robert.

Paint peeled from dilapidated houses that barely stood after years of neglect. Like relics from a nuclear disaster, they looked like warts rising up from the ground, destroying any hope of a beautiful neighborhood.

Trash littered the streets. Children played in playgrounds filled with broken wine and beer bottles.

Everywhere Bobby looked, a spirit of poverty hovered liked a brooding, sinister guard, keeping watch to make sure no one even thought of changing the way things were. But that suited Bobby just fine, at least for now. The decayed state of the eastside made for good business. Even the police didn't want to be there. Just a few more years, and he could make enough money to walk away. He fingered the long, platinum rope with the diamond-studded cross that hung from his neck. It was a symbol of all he'd accomplished and all he was going to accomplish—how he'd prove his teachers wrong. They said he wouldn't amount to much if he didn't get his grades up. But there were other ways to be successful besides college.

College.

He glanced at Robert. Robert was a college professor. Bobby hated the smug look on his stepfather's face every time he did something for the family. He hated the way Robert dressed and his cheap cologne that left his scent everywhere he went, like a dog urinating on a fire hydrant to mark his territory.

Still, being forced to hang around a college professor and listen to him rant had its benefits. Bobby had developed quite the vocabulary and picked up on some business skills that helped him on the street. Business he could handle. The street thugs were another story. But that was why he had Mike.

24

Robert made his quick stop. As he got back into the car, his irritating voice startled Bobby from his thoughts. "I'm so disappointed in you!"

Yeah, what else is new?

But Bobby didn't say anything. He watched the old, broken-down neighborhood where he used to live with his mother and older brother Justin, dissolve into the clean streets and beautiful lawns of the suburbs. It never ceased to amaze him how the neighborhoods transitioned from black and blight to clean and white. Just like that.

You could go on a walk here without someone sticking a gun in your face. The schools were new and big. This was Robert's 'hood. If Bobby had to give his stepdad credit for anything, it was bringing his family out of the darkness of the eastside and into the suburbs.

Bobby watched a family walking their dog down the street. Why couldn't his old neighborhood be like the suburbs? Why were so many of his old friends so dependent on the government to help them survive?

Robert's ranting about how ashamed he was of his stepson barely registered in Bobby's mind. It wasn't anything Bobby hadn't heard before, and he didn't care to hear it now. Especially from this man who thought he was the world to Bobby's family. Bobby rolled his eyes. The least Robert could have done was to bother to legally marry Bobby's mother. He hadn't.

But Bobby understood why his mother had hooked up with this man. Robert had been Mama's way out—her meal ticket.

Bobby rubbed his wrists again. He had a way out too. He would never rely on the government to take care of him. That's what he was doing on the streets with Mike and the others—making sure he could take care of himself. At least, that's how he saw it.

Apparently, Robert didn't agree.

"Don't you care about what this does to your mother and the shame you bring to this family?"

Bobby rubbed his forehead. It was getting harder to tune out Robert's voice. He couldn't wait to get home. Maybe he could disappear to his bedroom and find some peace. Wicked thoughts of how to get rid of Robert and make it look like an accident crept into his mind. He thought about it many times before but never had the courage to carry out such a devious deed. Selling drugs was one thing, getting rid of Robert was another. Finally, the two-story white house with aluminum siding came into view. Bobby hated that house about as much as he hated Robert. Every inch of it stank of the American Dream. The house wasn't anything like the houses he saw watching videos of his favorite rap stars. The only dream he had was getting out of this house and on his own for good. He opened the door and strode past the middle-class, fake furniture. He hurried to get upstairs as Robert was

26

kicking it into full gear. *If I can just make it to my room...*

Bobby made it past the baby pictures nailed to the wallpaper littered with pink flowers.

Almost there.

But it was too late. Robert was already sounding off like a drill sergeant. There would be no escape for Bobby today. "Get back here, boy!" Bobby trudged back to the living room. "This is the last time I'm coming down to that jail to get your behind out!" Robert's words dripped their usual condescension, like he was a real big man for having the resources to bail his stepson out of jail. "Next time, you can stay there until you learn how to act like a man!"

Bobby's mother rushed in and gave Bobby her standard emotional hug, like she hadn't seen him in twenty years. Then she started her usual crying, which always made things worse. Emma was always good for that. Bobby sighed. "It was only one day in jail, Mama." In his world, a day in jail wasn't enough to impress anyone who lived in the 'hood.

"Oh baby, I'm glad you're home." She sobbed like she had just lost her fur coat.

Her tears ran all over Bobby's shoulder. He fought the urge to roll his eyes. The Polo sweater he was wearing would never be the same.

After a minute, Mama pulled away and smiled through the tears. "I knew God would get you home."

Rage lit up Robert's eyes at the mention of God. Bobby cringed against it. Would his mama ever realize she couldn't pray Robert into church?

It would take more than faith to get that sinner saved.

"God?" Robert bellowed. "How about my money?" His dark, beady eyes bulged in their red-lined walls. "Do you understand how embarrassing it is for a professor of Black History to have to go down to the local jail to extricate his black son of a…" He stopped short of saying the b word. "…from the hands of some white man? A white man whose only joy is to see him locked up in the first place!"

He stopped short of saying the b-word so he wouldn't offend his wife's Christian sensitivities.

Emma put her hand on her Robert's arm. "Now Robert, not all white people are bad. There's plenty of 'bad' coming from other races too. And don't get so riled up. Bobby is still young."

Bobby knew the "still young" comment would set Robert off again. Robert rounded on Mama. "Young? Really? He's old enough to smoke that junk! And if you ask me, I think he's selling it! How else do you explain that necklace he's wearing?"

"I don't smoke that mess! And this necklace, as you call it, was a gift from a lady friend."

But Bobby knew that excuse would only go so far.

He was wearing his new True Religion jeans, even though they had been torn during his adventure with the police. His new shirt and new Air Force 1s loudly testified against him, too. He knew it would only be a matter of time before Robert and Mama would ask about those things.

If he were being honest, he hoped his mother would never learn where he spent most of his money. Memories flashed through his mind—the many times he 'made it rain' at the local strip club. Mama would be devastated if she knew.

Bobby glared at Robert.

I wonder if Robert knows where my money goes. Probably. Maybe that was it. Maybe he didn't like Robert because he knew Robert could see right through him. Maybe.

Then again, there were plenty of other reasons not to like Robert. Like the look of his rough face and the scratchy salt-and-pepper beard that needed trimming. Bobby hated the way he strutted as if he were royalty. Then there was Robert's hypocrisy. He had the audacity to pride himself on being a righteous man, but he never went to church. To Bobby, he was full of it.

"Why don't you back off, Robert?" Bobby stared down his stepdad. He knew Robert hated it when he called him by his first name. Robert stepped toward Bobby. He looked as though he wanted to hit him. Bobby stumbled one step backwards and dropped into an arm chair. Robert hovered over him like a storm cloud.

"You don't smoke? You know son, you don't do a lot of things. You don't go to school, you don't have a job, and you never read a book! Have you ever heard of John Hope Franklin? How about Jwanzaa Kunjufu? Or, maybe C. Eric Lincoln, or how about Mickey Mouse, or Donald Duck, or how about—"

Anger coursed through Bobby's veins. He jumped to his feet. "How about you just get up out of my face!" As if on cue, Bobby's grandmother shuffled into the room and stepped right between Robert and Bobby. Just her presence nearby soothed Bobby's raw nerves.

Thank God for Granny.

Granny squeezed Bobby in a tight hug. "There's my baby boy! You know I always miss you when you ain't here at the house. Bobby couldn't help but smile. Granny was nearly eighty-seven years old, but she could still put a pretty good bear hug on someone she liked.

"Hey, Granny. I tried to call you on my cell phone on the way home."

"Huh?" Granny cupped a hand to her ear. "What'd you say?"

Bobby raised his voice. "I said I called you on my cell phone on the way home."

30

Granny nodded knowingly. "Oh, yeah. There is a whole lot of hell in this home." She pursed her lips in a stern pout. "Sometimes I wonder if I should've just stayed in Alabama." She turned toward Robert and shot him a look that would've wilted the roses in her garden. "At least people in Alabama know who they are."

Bobby's mother stepped in now, and Bobby could've groaned aloud. She was about to stick up for Robert, just like she always did. Bobby couldn't help the pity that welled up inside when he looked at his mother. When had she traded her beauty and independence for the financial security Robert provided? Bobby used to believe love should matter. Now he realized money was far more important.

"Now, Mama, don't start on Robert today. God knows he's a whole lot better than this boy's daddy ever thought about being."

Her words felt like a slap to Bobby. How could she say that in front of Mr. Right? How could she tear down Bobby's father like that?

Robert didn't seem to appreciate his wife's help. "You don't have to fight my battles," he shouted. "This boy's rhetoric is quite innocuous to me. Bobby's behavior is simply endemic to his generation!"

"And what's that supposed to mean…*stepdaddy*?" Bobby glared at Robert in challenge.

Robert never missed an opportunity to put Bobby down. "What it means is you and your friends would rather spend the whole day watching those disgusting videos than read a book that might awaken the residuum of gray matter hopefully still in your head!"

Bobby opened his mouth to retaliate, but before he could get a word out, the front door opened and Justin walked in.

Justin—a breath of fresh air to Bobby, always. Bobby might have been jealous of Justin, older by one year. Justin was good-looking, intelligent, and loved singing in the church choir—everything Mama and Robert wanted in a son.

But Justin never judged Bobby, even though he knew Bobby had some problems. He saw the good in everyone and had always been there for his brother. Even now, Justin's eyes lit up when his gaze came to rest on Bobby.

"Bobby!"

"Hey, Justin." Bobby bumped shoulders with Justin in a traditional man-to-man hug. "What's up?"

"Gotta get ready for my choir rehearsal." Justin grinned. "We have a concert in a couple weeks. We could sure use your tenor voice, Bobby. You should think about it."

"Nah, I'm good."

Bobby ducked his head and wouldn't meet Justin's gaze.

"Well, I'll bet you're glad to be home. People gon' start calling you a convict!"

Bobby laughed. He glanced at Robert. Smoke might've started pouring from Robert's nostrils any second.

Granny scuttled back into the room with a piece of her famous Mississippi mud pie. The pie stirred up childhood memories for Bobby. He had always been confused about that name, mud pie. Why would they call it mud? It tasted pretty good to him.

In any case, Granny's soothing, motherly tone always lit that spark of hope inside Bobby. She smiled. "Here, I know you're hungry. Have something to eat. It's my Mississippi mud pie."

Bobby grinned, like he needed to be reminded. He dug into the pie and nudged Granny's elbow. "Hey, I thought you were from Alabama," he teased. Rich, dark crumbs of crust fell from his mouth.

"I was, till I moved to Mississippi. Shoot, when they started burnin' them crosses all up in my green grass, and stompin' all over my sunflowers, I knew it was time for me to go."

Robert folded his arms across his chest. "They did the same thing in Mississippi. I don't understand why you think that what white people did to blacks only happened in Alabama.

But Granny was too smart for Robert's phony posturing. She held her ear and leaned in toward him. "What did you say? You talkin' to me?"

Robert's distaste for Granny showed plainly on his face. He wrinkled his nose and looked at her like she might be an insect. Probably because Granny felt Robert wasn't good enough to be with Bobby's mama, and she didn't bother keeping it a secret.

But Robert didn't seem to want to let this one go. "I said they did the same thing in Mississippi, and now we are doing it to ourselves."

Mama frowned. "What do you mean, Robert?"

Bobby jumped in. "I know what he means. He's trying to say we're stomping on our own future— burning our own chances for success."

Robert's mouth fell open a little. But he recovered his wits quickly. "Why, that's exactly what I'm saying. That's impressive Bobby, but until you learn there's no hope in dope, and no jack in crack, you'll never amount to anything. You need to get educated!" *Nice attempt at spoken word, Robert. Uh, no.*

Maybe he could beat Robert at his own game. Bobby collected himself and pulled out every intelligent word he could remember. "You know, sagacious conversations in the average Black American family today are either non-existent, or at the very least, cantankerous and inciteful.

It is difficult at best, for me to justify any transmissions of thoughtful communications coming from you. Consequently, it would be far better to juxtapose your innocuous rancor with that of the inarticulate, cacophonic mumblings of the animal kingdom." The bewildered look that settled over Robert's face told it all.

Even Justin couldn't resist a rare stab at Robert. "Oops! I guess he told you."

Granny laughed. "And in your own language, too!"

It seemed like the only sympathy for Robert in the room was found with Bobby's mama. Again, she jumped to his rescue. "C'mon, Robert. Let me make you some coffee." She led him out of the room like he was a wounded warrior.

Relief washed over Bobby. It felt like he had been in a boxing match with the devil himself, and the bell had finally rung.

Justin's jovial demeanor returned. "Say, Bobby, don't you think you should lighten up a little on Daddy?"

Bobby didn't try to hide his disgust. "Daddy? How can you call him Daddy?" His anger toward Robert began to boil all over again.
"He don't know us. All he knows is his books. He don't know what it's like being out there, struggling to be somebody. I'm not going down like this!"

Justin leveled his gaze at Bobby. "You need to be careful, or you'll wind up in jail again. And don't forget, he didn't have to give us this home. I mean, would you take on a woman with two grown kids and a hard-of-hearing mother? That's like locking your own self in jail and throwing away the key. He loves Mama. He just has a hard time showing it."

Bobby's anger intensified. Rage now glowed inside. How could anyone not see through Robert?

Bobby grabbed Justin's arm, as if to shake some sense into him. "You don't see how he tries to control everything, Justin? Can't you see how he abuses Mama?"

Justin's eyebrows rose. He looked genuinely surprised. Maybe he truly didn't see the things that Bobby saw. Maybe he just didn't want to believe what he saw.

But Bobby was too angry to care. "We're supposed to be happy because he gave us a roof over our heads? Then, he demeans us under that same roof and pretends to be some educated hotshot! I don't think so!"

"Boys," Mama called from the dining room, "come eat some dinner." With a final glare at Justin's back, Bobby followed him to the table.

Bobby wolfed down his food. He couldn't seem to shake his irritation at his mother, and he didn't want her to see he depended on her for his sustenance. Why didn't she ever take his side over Robert?

He shoved the thought aside. It was probably foolish. Besides, he needed to meet up with his friends, Mike and Tina. Best to hurry through this meal and duck out as quickly as possible.

Mama frowned at him from across the table. "Bobby!" Her voice carried that nagging tone. "Why are you gulping your food down so fast?"

Bobby jumped up and grabbed his jacket. He was already late for his rendezvous with Mike and Tina and didn't feel like answering his mama's questions.

But his mother jumped up and stood directly in his path. "Where do you think you're off to?"

"Here we go again. Round seven." Bobby fought his emotions, trying to control the disrespect in his voice. "Mama, why are you always getting on my case?"

"Getting on your case?" She went from Sister Emma, the church lady, to Mama, in two seconds flat. Her eyes blazed, then squinted shut. The lines on her face deepened with anger. "What's that supposed to mean?"

"Mama! Can't I just come in here and eat this nasty food in peace for a change? What do you expect from me, a dissertation or something?"

He knew he'd stepped out of line with her. But he couldn't help himself as his emotions bubbled over.

He didn't know how she would respond. Fortunately, she took the high road. For now.

She dug her fists into her hips. "Look, all I asked was a simple question, and all I expect from yo' narrow behind is a simple answer! Pastor Smith was just preaching about the last days and people giving in to seducing spirits and doctrines of devils."

"Here you go again with Pastor said this and Pastor said that. I mean, Mama, don't that little raggedy Bible you always reading, say something like, 'Thou shalt have no other god before me'? You can't make a god out of that man 'cause he pass gas, just like everybody else!"

"God don't pass no gas!" Granny corrected him as she adjusted her ear piece.

Robert appeared in the doorway, apparently drawn by the noisy rhetoric. He looked ready to attack; Bobby wished he could just make himself disappear. Sure enough, Robert wasted no time. "The Bible also says obey them that have rule over you! Now answer the question!"

Bobby's emotions stirred in his gut. It was time—time to finally stand up to the man. He lifted his head high and looked Robert right in his angry, contorted face. "What's the big deal?"

"What do you mean, what's the big deal?" Robert snarled.

"About where I'm going. That's my business. But if it pleases you, Puffy Daddy, I'm going to meet Mike and Tina."

Bobby knew that remark would pull his mother back into the fight. She never liked any of his friends and always thought they were just hood rats and heathens, on their way to Hell.

"I should've known!" Mama's eyes flashed. "You still hanging out with those two good-for-nothing friends of yours!"

To Mama, all his friends were good-for-nothing. She never took the time to know them. As far as Bobby was concerned, she was just trippin'. Why did parents seem to think that their kids' lives were about them?

Bobby prepared himself for another attack from Mama, and it came quickly.

"Don't you know we're living in Perilous Times?" She moved closer to him, her voice pleading now. "Listen sweetheart, the streets are dangerous. drugs, guns, AIDS. I just want you to think for a minute." Tears welled in her eyes. "Why don't you stay home tonight? We can all talk about how we're going to make things better. I know God has something better for you. You just need to go back and finish school. It's not God's will that you wind up in jail or living with your girlfriend, like that Mike and Tina!"

At the mention of Mike and Tina, her tears evaporated and her eyes blazed fire.

Bobby felt like she stuck a knife in him. His anger spewed out disrespectfully. "Dang! Now who told you that, Mama? Everybody knows where you get it from—the same place all the gossip comes from. The church! Y'all just sit around, running other folks down, especially when y'all in a restaurant eating chicken! Don't forget, Mama, your tongue is a weapon too!"

Robert stepped up, his fists balled at his sides. "And your tongue is about to get you in a world of trouble. Now, you say you have somewhere to go? I think you better be going, because I'm not going to stand here and listen to you talk to your mother like this!"

"Well sit, then!" Bobby shot back.

Robert moved toward him. His brows pulled down over his eyes like a threatening storm.

"Bobby!" Mama screamed. "Robert!" She grabbed Robert's arm.

She obviously knew Robert was about to explode. Bobby knew it, too. Wouldn't be the first time Robert had gone off.

Mama pushed against Robert. "Robert, that's just the devil talking. You can't let it bother you!" Her eyes swam, deep and troubled. Things were unraveling and she knew it.

Time to get out of here.

Bobby turned to his mother. "You know what, Mama?

40

I'm gone, and maybe I'm gone for good this time!
'Cause this house ain't big enough for the both of us!"

Mama let go of Robert and grabbed onto Bobby.
"Bobby, wait a minute!"

"Emma! Let the boy go!" Robert's shout nearly
shook the windows.

"No, Robert!" Then she turned to Bobby,
desperation written all over her face. "Now, Bobby,
listen to me baby…"

"No, Mama. It's either him or me! I can't take it
anymore. It's time to leave."

Justin, who'd been silent this whole time, huffed
and stomped away toward his room. Robert's voice hit
a new volume. "Get out of my house!"

Bobby didn't budge an inch. He just stared at his
stepfather.

"I said get out of my house!"

Bobby's mother clutched a hand to her chest.
Her gaze darted from her husband to her son like she
was watching some evil spirit rip her household apart,
and there was nothing she could do about it. "Robert,
please…"

But Robert wasn't having any of it. "Let him go,
Emma!" Robert's voice was loud enough to stir
Granny. She always did hate shouting.

Granny jumped up from her seat and stood
courageously in front of Robert pointing a finger at

him. "The blood of Jesus! The blood of Jesus! Hallelujah!"

She made that phrase sound like it was some kind of magical word. But by now, Robert was ready to confront anyone standing in his way. He seemed empowered by the force that had overtaken the home.

"Sit down, Mother!"

Even Mama seemed surprised by Robert's ugly tone. "Don't talk to Mother like that. She doesn't mean any harm."

Bobby had enough of the whole mess. Neither of his parents was going to understand him. After all, what did they know about his generation and what they were going through? They didn't know anything about his frustration, his peer pressure, and his need to be accepted. They didn't understand his world. It was as simple as that.

Bobby tried to calm the storm inside him. He forced some composure and turned to his sobbing mother. "It's better this way." He moved toward the door. "I'm sorry about my temper. I guess I got that from my *real* father."

Mama suddenly looked ten years older. She grabbed Bobby by both arms, eyes desperate. "Where are you going?"

"Where I want to go."

"What are you going to do?"

"What I want to do!"

The questions kept coming, one after another. "Well, who you going to be with, honey?"

Before he could answer, Mr. Professor chimed in. "I'm sure he'll find a room with Ike and Tina Turner, or whatever their names are."

The flippant remark from Robert stopped Bobby in his tracks. He fired back. "That's right. Somebody who actually loves me!"

"Love? What do you know about love?" Robert moved in for the kill. "You think love is all those women parading around on those videos you watch day and night, shaking their behinds because their brains are asleep! You think love is spending your money on some girl swinging around half-naked on a pole, telling you things to make you feel like a man! You think love is putting a big platinum cross around your neck and calling yourself Ludacross!"

"It's Ludacris!"

"Ludacris, Ludacross, it's all the same thing!"

Veins bulged in Robert's neck, and his eyes looked darker than ever. He had a cold glare in his gaze, like he could kill somebody. How could a person look like that while talking about the cross?

But Bobby knew Robert was telling him the truth about the girls and the money and the diamond cross.

And Robert wasn't done with his attack.

"You have no idea what that cross stands for. Your generation thinks you're the man, you've arrived, and you're hot. Well, one day you'll find out just what that cross means."

"And so will you!" Bobby snapped back.

Mama stepped in, new determination on her face. She looked ready to take control of the situation. "Okay, Bobby, that's enough! He may not be your real father, but you're going to respect him. And remember, I am still your mother!"

"Well, happy Mother's Day!" Bobby shouted. "Today y'all gon' learn how to respect me, 'cause I'm a grown man!"

His words sounded tough and disrespectful, and they made him feel grown. But this pseudo-macho moment only lasted for a few seconds, because his mother wasn't deterred. She came at him with a tone that said she wasn't playing games.

"Oh, you say so, huh? Well, let me tell you something. I brought your little tail into this world, and baby, I will take you out!" She whacked him as hard as she could with her shoe.

Bobby barely moved, but with every blow, his anger grew.

Mama hollered at him, her voice shrilled. "You act like you've lost your mind!"

"You know what, Mama? I've had it with you! You don't know what you want.

But I know what I want. I'm not a fool!

Robert drew himself up to his full height. Bobby had a sinking feeling things were about to get real crazy. His stepdad looked like one of the snarling pit bulls that had chased him before. "So, you're not a fool, huh?"

"Are you deaf and dumb?"

Robert's eyes lit up like fire at Bobby's incendiary question. He moved a step closer to his young adversary, face-to-face, so that he was practically spitting on him. "Boy, do you see this woman right here? That's my queen! You and nobody else—" But before he could continue, Mama grabbed him, trying to restrain him. Like a ravenous lion, he looked at her and roared, "Woman, let me go!"

Bobby felt the house shake and rattle. It was something he had experienced only once before when his parents argued. Mama's eyes popped wide as Robert turned back to Bobby.

He ranted on. "As I said, you and nobody else is going to—"

Mama grabbed him again. "Robert, please!"

He turned to her with a look in his eyes like a crazed bull. "Woman, if you grab me one more time to take up for this fake wanna-be…"

The lights in the house started blinking and a strange wind whistled through the room.

Bobby's instinct to protect his mother kicked in. "Hey, you need to chill with my mama!"

He, not Robert, was the man of the house. And he was ready to show them all.

But before Bobby could say anything else, Robert charged toward him, nostrils flared. Bobby's heart leaped into his throat as Robert came at him like a demon straight from Hell. Robert's belligerent shouting filled the room. "You're not so big I can't whoop your behind!" He slammed Bobby to the floor like a heavyweight wrestler, then positioned himself to pound Bobby into the next life. Bobby caught flashes of his mother's and Granny's faces. They'd come to his rescue and seemed to be jumping on his crazed attacker.

"Get off me!" Robert shouted at the women. For a moment, the professor lost his dignity and his propensity to use proper language. "Y'all gon' make me lose my mind up in here!" He struggled to get the women off him.

That was Bobby's chance to get away.

He got up and stumbled to the other side of the room like a drunk in the streets. Robert spotted a chair and went after it, apparently ready to use it to knock Bobby further into submission. But before he could grab it, Granny beat him there and sat in it.

Robert screamed at her. "I don't need a chair!"

Eyes bulging, he came after Bobby with his fists raised. Just like he had a few nights before when he hit Bobby's mother. This time, it was Bobby's turn to stand face-to-face.

46

"Go ahead! Slap me like you slapped my mama the other night!"

Robert froze in his tracks as though the world suddenly ended. His embarrassed face was weak and expressionless until he sucked in his jaws as if searching for something to say. He stumbled back a step.

Bobby glared at him. "Yeah, you lookin' stupid now. I know about you. The whole freakin' neighborhood knows about you, Robert!"

Justin reappeared from his bedroom. His eyebrows rose and his mouth dropped when he took in the scene—the horror on his mother's face, Granny wiping her tearing eyes. "What's going on in here? Can't anybody here recognize the presence of the devil! The house is going nuts. Lights blinking, wind blowing, roof shaking."

Bobby gestured to Robert. "Big Daddy Kane is trippin' up in here!"

Silence fell over the room. Justin looked at Robert, and Bobby could almost hear the conflict raging inside him—like he was about to say something he'd wanted to say for a long time but was hoping he'd never have to.

Finally, Justin spoke. "Look, Pops, I don't know what your problem is, but we ain't kids no more, you know what I'm sayin'? You put your hands on my mama one more time, I guarantee you, me and Bobby gon' put a serious hurting on you!"

Robert visibly recoiled from Justin's words.

But Justin didn't stop. "We're supposed to be family, and you're supposed to be the head. But you're running around here like, 'I'm the man, show me some respect!' Well, you got to give it to get it! You're supposed to be intelligent and educated. What educated man would beat his own wife?"

Robert reached out to Bobby, as if he was apologizing. "Listen, I'm sorry."

Bobby shrank back from Robert's approach. "Don't touch me! Ain't no love in this joint! That's why I do my thing in the street."

Emma began to cry. Granny put her arms around her daughter, trying to comfort her.

Justin dropped his head into his hands for a moment. His shoulders drooped and his whole posture spelled defeat. "We heard Mama crying and we heard her praying. She was asking God to change your ways." Justin lifted his head, and anger flashed in his eyes. "I don't understand why you do it!" The tears he was holding back began to flow and he stormed toward his room.

Robert stared after him, a furrow creasing his brow like he didn't understand. "Justin, I love your mother!" Robert called out.

But it wasn't enough.

Justin's door slammed down the hall. He obviously didn't want to hear any more.

Robert turned and looked at his wife as if he was looking for someone to console him. He walked toward her, cautiously, and gently put his arm around her.

She seemed to shrink at his touch. Bobby barely heard her speak. "Not now, Robert."

Robert tried to catch her gaze. "Every time I try to show you love, you turn me away." His words held a note of desperation.

"I turn you away?" her reply darted back at him. "Robert, you have turned me away for nearly five years now! All you do is sit around and read your books. You never stop to take time to ask the boys what they're going through. You've never taken them fishing, or even told them anything about how to deal with life. The world is different now. Kids today have real problems, just like adults. They don't know what real love is because they never see it at home!"

Hurt and anger lit up her features, though the tears flowed freely down her face. Bobby had never seen her talk back to Robert like this. "When was the last time you brought me flowers other than Valentine's Day? When was the last time you kissed me in front of the boys? When was the last time you went to church with us?" She stopped for a moment, still sobbing. "You don't love me."

Robert pulled back from her, shock written all over his face. "It's not that, honey.

You know I'm committed to you. I love you and I know things will work out. I've always loved you, since the moment I first saw you. You remember when we first met at the supermarket? Remember? You had lost your keys and I helped you find them. I fell in love with you when you thanked me with those beautiful eyes. I do love you. I just have a difficult time getting over my past hurts. When I lost my wife..."

Bobby's mother cut him off. "You don't have to say any more." she said softly.

Bobby could have groaned out loud. Robert's words were melting her heart—as usual. This is what he always did. He was convincing when he had to be and knew exactly what to say to make her give in.

She took Robert's hand, her eyes serious, but all the anger evaporated. "Just promise me, no more fighting. I can't love you if I'm afraid of you."

"I promise."

"Lies, all lies!" Granny's voice boomed across the room. Her ears seemed to be working perfectly at the moment. She lit into both of them. "I dun seen it all! Y'all too ghetto for me. Y'all need to be on Jerry Springer, or something. Maybe Judge Mathis can help y'all!" And with that, like Justin, she too stormed out the room.

"Things will be different, won't they Robert?" Bobby saw the confused and almost child-like look on Mama's face.

He patted her hand. "Of course they will."

I know, I haven't been the best to you
Never altogether true, but oh, my love, I'm trying
I know, there are little things that I can do
To make a change for me and you
But oh, my love, I'm still trying
The hand that I was dealt seems so unfair
I don't have a friend that even cares
But that's no excuse for the abuse that I've given you
But I promise you, I'll keep trying till I get it right
So give me the chance to renew the romance with you
Honey, you are my queen and I'll do anything for you
I know, I haven't been the best for you
I tried so hard to make it true
But oh, my love, I'm trying
I know that we can make it if we say
I love you honey, day by day
With God's help, we can make it
I know that there are times that we may be down
But we can't afford to carry a frown
We got to confess we have the best in ourselves
So I promise you I'll keep trying till I get it right
So give me the chance to renew the romance with you
Honey, you are my king and I'll do anything for you

Robert and Mama stood there hugging each other as if nothing had happened. The storm had passed, at least for now.

Bobby always hated this part. They were fooling themselves to think that anything would change. He had seen this story over and over. All it took was a few words from Robert and everything was back to normal.

Justin emerged from his room with his backpack loaded with clothes.

Emma rose to her feet. "Justin, where are you going?"

"You don't understand what I'm going through, Mama. Every night, it's the same thing. You fight, you make up, and then you fight again. I'm sorry, but I can't take it anymore." He raced out the door. Bobby gave both Robert and his mother a long glare, then followed after Justin.

And just like that, both boys were gone.

Just like that, the family was split up. Just like that, the enemy had won…again.

C h a p t e r   2

Trouble in the Streets

Bobby squirmed in an overstuffed armchair. He was supposed to hook up with Mike and Tina, but after he caught up with his brother, Justin convinced him to hang out at his friend's house. Justin's friend, Darreon, was a church boy. He and his sister Isis, always talked about prayer and how things can change after a person talks to God. Bobby had been there all of five minutes, and already he felt uncomfortable enough to crawl out of his skin. Didn't seem he could escape church people, no matter where he went.

Darreon smiled. "You guys want something to drink? My mom can fix some food if you're hungry. I know God will work things out for both of you".

Bobby couldn't take it anymore. He jumped up from his chair. "Hey, I have to go back home for a minute." His brain scrambled for a believable lie. "I left my wallet."

"I'll go back with you." Justin frowned. "It might not be a good idea for you to go alone."

"No, I'm good." Bobby was already halfway out the door. "No stress on my end."

"Ok." Justin still didn't look convinced. "Call me as soon as you can. I'll be waiting."

"Yeah."

But the moment Bobby's shoes touched the sidewalk, he headed in the direction opposite his former home. Managing to hitchhike a ride along the way, he headed toward Belle Isle—the place where he, Mike, and Tina often hooked up.

Belle Isle is a small island just off the Detroit River. It was a cool place to meet because all you had to do was make it look like you were having a picnic and no one would bother you. It was the place they took care of a lot of their business.

It was Bobby's favorite spot, and not just because it was a prime business location. He'd gone there a lot as a kid, too. His mama loved going there to fire up a grill for family reunions, back when things were so much fun for Bobby and Justin.

Hundreds of beautiful red and yellow flowers lined the structures there. Weeping willows, which hung low by the banks of the park's small lakes and ponds, were especially meaningful to Bobby. They always reminded him of his dad's funeral. Even though it was sad, he liked the reminder.

And then there were the huge cargo ships. As long as Bobby could remember, he loved watching the ships float by. Bobby's father said his high school football and track teams used to practice at Belle Isle because his school didn't have a field.

54

Dad used it for sports; Bobby used it for money, whether or not the flowers bloomed or ships sailed by. Time had changed all things, Bobby supposed.

Some of Bobby's other boys were already there, Jacob and Drew, just hanging out. They had opened the back hatches of their SUVs, brought out some food, and sat around watching the cars that went by waiting for some business to drop in. Tina was sporting some blue pants that were super tight, as usual. Her clothing always matched her long, decorative nails and her shoes.

She always looked sweet, and her swaying ponytail, which ended halfway down her back, caught every guy's attention, including Bobby's. Although her overall stature was small, her words were big and bold.

Mike was lucky to have her. Bobby knew Mike didn't realize Tina had a thing for him. She admired his intelligence. If Mike had known, he wouldn't have kept it a secret. He would have been furious, at both Tina and Bobby.

What he don't know won't hurt him.

But it didn't matter anyway. Tina made no secret of the fact that money was her number one passion. And Mike, who made much more money than Bobby did, was more connected to the 'man', he knew how to work the streets of Detroit better, so Tina stayed with him.

As Bobby approached them, he could already see displeasure etched into Mike's face. Mike was always angry when Bobby was late. "Disrespectful to the business." he always said.

Mike took a long drag on a blunt that had nearly disappeared between his blackened fingertips, not seeming to care it was broad daylight. In his mind the police barely cared, so, why should he?

He frowned at Bobby. "What took you so long, Bobby? Your old man bailed you out more than three hours ago. I know this because I checked up on you."

Bobby cringed at the idea of telling Mike of the family squabbles. "Nothing."

"Nothing? LJ's all on my back about the money you owe him and you walkin' around here like ain't nothing going on? What's up with that? I don't understand you, man." Mike's eyebrows rose until they disappeared under his hat. "This is a business! With everybody out here buying and selling, we're losing a lot of business. LJ's countin' on you!"

Bobby tried not to shudder at the thought of LJ—and the money he owed him. "So, where's LJ now?"

"I'm sure he's at the club, probably counting his loot from last night, and realizing you're short on what you owe him." Mike shot Bobby a pointed glare.

"Look man, I'm a little short, but you know I'm good for it."

56

Mike's face didn't soften. He pressed his index finger into Bobby's forehead. "Man, those few hours in jail must have affected your brain. You know LJ ain't going for that!"

Tina pranced up to Bobby with a flirtatious grin on her face. "So, how much you short Bobby, 'cause I do have a little extra cash, and it's yours if you want it." She leaned toward his face.

Her perfume had a definite effect on his equilibrium. She didn't seem to care that Mike was standing there, and for the moment, neither did Bobby. "You'd do that for me?" he said, trying to keep his voice cool.

"I sure would, and a whole…lot…more." She punctuated her words as she toyed with Bobby's collar.

Then she glanced back at Mike. It was pretty obvious she was trying to make him jealous. Bobby wondered if that had to do with the fact that a couple hotties had been hanging out with Mike at the club a few nights before.

Mike's face darkened further. "I know she didn't say what I thought she said."

"That's what she said!" everyone hollered back.

Mike stood there, disbelief plain in his eyes. He turned back to Tina. "Well, what did you say?"

It sounded like a test to Bobby. One last chance to change her statement and fall back in step, where Mike wanted her.

But Tina seemed to want to show off how bold and sassy she could be. She walked up to Mike with her neck popping in concert with her curvaceous figure. "I said, I got a little extra cash for my boy Bobby. Cause you see, I work hard for my money, baby!"

Bobby braced himself. Mike would have to respond in the strongest way possible, with everyone watching. Bobby knew Mike wouldn't let Tina front him off like that.

Mike looked at Tina with a sharp eye. He paused for a moment, almost like he was making sure everyone was looking. "I thought that's what you said." Out of nowhere, his hand came smashing into her face knocking her to the ground.

An image of Mama and Robert flashed through Bobby's mind—not just an image, but a memory. Bobby wanted to go to Tina—to help her. But she was Mike's girl.

Tina's hand flew to her jaw. Tears streamed down her face, but for a moment, she just sat there, apparently in shock. Then, she jumped to her feet. "One of these days, you're gonna learn how to treat a woman like a woman!"

"Well, baby, today ain't that day." Mike pushed her into Bobby's arms. "Take her. She's yours. She don't deserve a sweet thang like me!" The look he gave Bobby felt like a warning. "I'll see you at the club tonight. Don't be late, and don't forget LJ's looking for you, so you better get up on the rest of that money!"

The night seemingly came within minutes for Bobby, and he still didn't have all of LJ's money. He regretted buying new clothes with LJ's money. When he walked into the club, everyone was partying, dancing, and doing their usual thing, except Tina. She was still boiling with anger, holding a cold towel over the red contusion on her face. She wanted to make sure everyone knew Mike had hit her.

Bobby's eyes surveyed the room not knowing what to expect from LJ, or Mike, for that matter. Mike never forgot a confrontation and always looked for an opportunity to be like LJ, tough, and with money.

The lights in the club were low but bright enough to highlight the haze of cigarette and marijuana smoke. Some were drinking beer while others were busy trying to look like they were 'all that' by throwing down some vodka or some other mixed drink.

The girls were barely dressed. Some wore skirts that showed everything a guy wanted to see, others wore jeans or leggings so tight you had to wonder how they even got into them. The guys had on their True Religion jeans and Polo shirts, their hats cocked to the side or backwards. There was so much ice around their necks and wrists, they could have opened up their own jewelry business. Bobby knew one day he would have everything they had, and more. But for now, he had to be concerned about his debt to LJ.

As some of the women approached him, he suddenly heard his brother's voice. "Bobby, Bobby! I need to speak to you!" Justin shouted.

Before Bobby could say a word to Justin, Snake, the club bouncer, walked up to Justin and grabbed him by the collar. Which was easy to do, since Snake was about 6'5 and three hundred pounds.

"Say, young blood, you got some ID?"

Bobby knew Snake was ready to throw Justin out, so he stepped in, "Hey Snake, this is my brother. He's cool."

"I don't care if he's the president. If he ain't got no ID, he's got to get up outta here!"

Bobby desperately pushed Justin toward the door. "Look Justin, this ain't no place for you. You need to go on back home."

Images flashed through Bobby's mind—Justin graduating from college, maybe going on to law school or medical school. He was too good a person to be in this club. The last thing Bobby wanted was for Justin to follow down the path he had chosen.

He redoubled his efforts to push Justin toward the door. "Look man, I'm telling you, you need to go home. You can't be here. You don't know these people!"

"Bobby, I'm not going back home. I'm tired of their fussin' and cussin', and then making up like nothing ever happened. I can't take it anymore.

I made up my mind. We're in this thing together. I'm sorry you were so uncomfortable earlier. Listen, I'm hanging with you."

Bobby's heart sank to his sneakers. "Look, Justin. I love you man. You're my brother. But I can't let you come here. It's too dangerous. Besides, I don't even know where I'm staying tonight."

He glanced at Mike, who was only a few feet away listening to every word between the brothers.

Before Justin could respond, one of the girls from the club walked up to them, flashing everything she could. Bobby had to admit that the girl was beautifully put together. Her long, dark hair flowed gently down her back, complimenting all the curves she either bought or was naturally blessed with. Judging by the way Justin's face lit up, he seemed to be enjoying the attention she gave him. A stupid grin stretched across his mouth as he watched her move.

After tossing a flirtatious smile in Justin's direction, she turned to Bobby. "Hey, Bobby, your brother is kinda cute! Why don't you hook a sista' up. I like 'em smart and strong." A smirk twisted her lips. "I heard you need some money. How 'bout I give you a hundred dollars for your brother?" she laughed.

Bobby's temper rose in a heartbeat. "How 'bout I go upside your head!"

Mike stepped in like a fireman putting out a blaze. "Man, why don't you lighten up.

She's just joking! What's the problem, Bobby? You uptight 'cause you ain't got all of LJ's money? Is that the problem? You feeling kinda nervous?"

Bobby ignored him for the moment and turned back to his brother. "Look J, this ain't the place for you. You need to leave. Things will work out at home; you just need to hang in there."

Mike interrupted. "Tell you what, Bobby. I'll give you a couple hundred for what you've been doing for me, but you gotta get up on the rest, and I want mine back in two weeks. Now, I think you better get lost for a minute unless you want to deal with LJ tonight. I'll tell him you got a grand and you're out workin' to get the rest."

Bobby glanced at Justin. He didn't want to show weakness in front of his brother. "I'm not running from LJ or anybody else." His words sounded harder—and braver—than he felt.

Before he knew it, Snake walked over to him. "Say homeboy, LJ wants to see you."

"Who, me?"

"Yeah, you! I told him you was in the house."

Bobby trudged slowly through the club, like a death march. The knot in his stomach tightening every time he thought about his confrontation with LJ.

The club was now packed with beautiful young girls shaking their behinds on stage.

The dollars floated through the air as the guys tossed them at their young entertainment. The whole scene reminded Bobby of Robert's words, "…girls shaking their behinds because their brains are asleep."

But Bobby quickly dismissed the thought when Snake opened the door to LJ's back room. There he sat with two half-dressed women on either side of him. He was puffing on a cigar which made him seem older, although he was only twenty-five. The big diamonds on his watch glittered like tiny lightbulbs, and these were accompanied by a pinky ring that was worth at least $20,000.

When Bobby approached LJ, he knew he would have to suck up to him a bit.

"Hey LJ, what's up man?" He put out his hand but LJ ignored it.

Bobby tried again, "What's good, LJ? Hey, check it out. You know that deal we had over on the Boulevard?"

Bobby was talking very fast, and he knew it. But LJ didn't seem to be buying it.

LJ ignored Bobby's question and glared. "You got my money Bobby?"

"Yeah, I got your money."

Some of it…

He tried to get LJ's mind off the money. "Man, the club is jumping tonight!" Bobby knew that his rhetoric double-talk wasn't working.

63

LJ stood up, all six feet seven inches of him hovering over Bobby. "I don't want to talk about the club. Do you have my money?"

Bobby took a couple steps back. "Okay, look man, I'm not gon' play you. I'm here…but all the money ain't."

"What do you mean you're here, but all the money ain't?" The storm already brewing on LJ's face darkened further.

Bobby's heart tripped, then hammered in his ribcage. What would LJ do to him?

Before Bobby could piece together a coherent response, Justin walked into the room. LJ's gaze bounced from Justin to Snake, then back to Justin.

LJ nodded to Justin. "So, who is this, Bobby, your bodyguard?"

"He's my brother." Bobby could barely manage the words. "He just came up to tell me about some problems at home. My mother is pretty sick."

But the look on LJ's face told it all. He wasn't buying this story, and the lie only made him angrier. Bobby had a sinking feeling something bad was about to go down.

LJ stepped into Bobby's face. "What's up with this? You bought your brother some shoes or something, Bobby? You paid your mama's tithes at church with my money? How you gon' play me? I do everything in the world for you Bobby!

64

I give you anything you want. If I let you get away with this, every punk in Detroit gon' be trying to play me!" By now, everyone else could hear the commotion. It was obvious something was about to happen. It was a scene they were all familiar with.

LJ looked at Bobby in disgust. "Slap yourself, fool!"

Bobby felt his mouth drop open. "What?"

"I said, slap yourself!"

Bobby glanced around at the onlookers. "C'mon, LJ, don't do this."

"I said slap yourself. Now!"

Bobby figured he'd better do what LJ said, no matter how embarrassing it was. He lifted his hand and slapped his own face. Everybody burst into laughter. Bobby felt like sinking through the floor or making himself disappear. Anything to get out of this ridiculous situation.

But LJ wasn't finished. "Grab your butt, Bobby." LJ raised his voice so no one would be able to avoid hearing his command.

"LJ, c'mon, man. I'll get your money. Please. You don't have to do this."

"I said, grab your butt!" LJ shouted again.

Bobby sighed, but he grabbed his butt. Maybe this would end the humiliation.

LJ sneered. "See right there, that's what you are to me. A pain in the butt!"

Bobby motioned for LJ to follow him over to a remote part of the room.

Maybe he could get the big man to quiet down and convince him he was still his boy. But LJ still wasn't buying. He stood his ground, never budging an inch. The fear in Bobby expanded until he couldn't seem to feel or think anything else. He had already heard how one guy, a year ago, had been in a similar situation. He was only short about $200. After the guy met in LJ's office, no one ever saw him again. At least not until they found him floating in the Detroit River.

Bobby couldn't let that happen. "LJ, all I need is a couple more days. I swear to you, I'll have the rest of the money soon."

But LJ simply turned away and went back to his desk, making sure that everyone could see he was the big man. The boss. "A couple more days, huh? You need a couple more days with my money?"

"Yeah, just a couple more days. I swear I'm good for it!" Bobby knew he was in big trouble. He knew it was practically a sin to mess with LJ's money. He scolded himself momentarily. *Why was I so stupid!* He looked at the platinum chain that hung loosely around his neck for everyone to see. The chain and the clothes could have waited.

"LJ, I—"

But Bobby was cut off by LJ spinning back around. Bobby heard screams and sensed movement all around him. But all he could feel was the cold, metallic bite of the .45 caliber LJ had pressed to his forehead. Out of the corner of his eye, Bobby saw Justin take a couple steps toward him. But two of LJ's thugs grabbed Justin. Though he struggled, they proved too strong.

The barrel of the gun pressed hard against Bobby's skull. Terror raced through him. Would he pass out before LJ pulled the trigger? He stole a glance at Justin. Was there any way both of them would survive the night? How had he managed to get his brother involved in this dilemma? Guilt throbbed in his chest, nearly blotting out the terror.

LJ shouted above the chaos in the club. "Give me a reason why I shouldn't blow you away!" Bobby's heart pounded in his ears. What should he say?

He dropped to his knees. "I just got a job. I'm gonna get the money to you. I swear."

LJ laughed. "Seriously? You can do better than that, Bobby. Give me a reason and give it to me *now*!"

Bobby's mind raced. "I ain't never been shot before!" he blurted.

A chorus of laughter broke out from Snake and the rest of the guys around him.

It was a stupid thing to say, Bobby knew it. But for a moment, Bobby thought that even LJ might find it funny and lighten up. The next minute would tell. The next minute would determine his fate. The next minute everything could change. Bobby braced himself and tried to steady his thoughts.

Will I go to Heaven or Hell if I die? Will God forgive me of my sins? Will anyone show up at my funeral, besides my family?

The thoughts clamored for position in his mind, unbidden. He couldn't seem to still them.

"Okay, you wanna play games, huh?" barked LJ. He put the gun away.

Bobby let out his breath in a low, slow exhale.

"Tell you what, Bobby, we all gon' play a game. This here is called heads or tails. Snake! Give me a quarter!"

Snake tossed a quarter to LJ. Bobby's gaze stayed glued to the silver coin.

LJ held it up. "Okay Bobby, heads you win, tails you lose."

So much for the easy breathing. Bobby's throat tightened and his heart hammered like it would jump out his chest.

Without meaning to, Bobby muttered a prayer under his breath. "Please let it be heads...please God, let it be heads. I need your help Lord. Don't let me go down like this."

But would God answer? Bobby wasn't convinced.

So, he tried LJ one more time. "LJ, I put my life on the line for you!"

"And I paid you, man. I paid you every time you was out there!"

The cross that dangled around Bobby's neck flashed before him, and Robert's words came ringing back: "One day you'll find out what that cross means."

LJ flipped the quarter high in the air. It seemed like the world had slowed as the coin flipped end-over-end through the air and back into LJ's palm.

Snake leaned over LJ's shoulder to look. "It's tails."

No.

LJ reached for his gun.

Last chance.

Bobby pulled back his fist. Then he punched LJ square on the nose with all his strength. His feet barely managed to stay beneath him as he scrambled for the door.

Bobby turned to yell over his shoulder. "C'mon J! C'mon J! Run! Run!"

Bobby couldn't see how it'd happened, but Justin cut loose from the two thugs. He pulled up alongside Bobby, and they pushed hard for the exit.

Streetlight illuminated the doorframe. Bobby could almost smell the fresh air outside. They were close. They were going to make it. They were going to be free.

Then two shots rang out.

Bobby didn't want to look back, but he had to. He *knew* he had to. The smoke cleared slowly. In its wake, a lifeless figure lay on the floor.

Justin.

Bobby's heart felt like it crashed into his shoes. "J?" He started to bend down—was his brother still breathing?

But then LJ's voice grabbed his attention. "Take him out! Take that fool out!"

Bobby glanced up to see Snake taking out his gun, which for a moment was somehow stuck in the holster. This was his only opportunity—his last hope. He had to leave, with or without Justin.

He took off into the crisp, Detroit night. Through the streets of the city, past the neighborhoods he sold drugs in, past people who knew he was in trouble. He ran without seeing anything, except Justin's limp body crumpled to the floor.

When Bobby's lungs felt ready to burst, he skidded to a stop in an alleyway. He reached into his pocket for his cell phone, but it wasn't there. He must have dropped it in the scuffle.

"Hey," he managed to choke out to a lady passing by the alley. "Can I borrow your cell phone? It's an emergency."

The lady eyed him warily, but then she handed over her phone.

Bobby dialed 911.

"911, what's your emergency?"

"My brother's been shot!" Bobby gave the dispatcher the name and location of the club.

70

"We'll send an ambulance. Sir, are you hurt? Are you in trouble?"

Bobby hung up and handed the phone back to the wide-eyed lady. "Thanks."

Before she could ask him any questions, he took off running again. Back to the aluminum-sided houses and the fake, middle-class furniture. Back to the safety of the suburbs.

Honor your Father and Mother...
Fathers, don't exasperate your
children by coming down hard on
them...Eph 6:2,4

Chapter 3

The Fork in the Road

His house was finally in sight, and it was a good thing. Bobby's legs were giving out, and so was his wind. When he burst through the door, Mama and Robert were sitting at the table having a cup of coffee. Bobby tried to brush past them into his bedroom, but they both turned and noticed that he was breathing hard and sweating.

Mama didn't skip a beat. "Where have you been, and where is your brother?"

Bobby didn't respond. He couldn't.

His mother frowned. "What's wrong with you boy? You're shaking like a leaf." Silence. "I said, what's wrong with you?"

Bobby slumped in a nearby chair and dropped his head in his hands. He couldn't hold it in any longer. Tears spilled from his eyes and rolled down his face.

Robert's voice held no sympathy. "I thought you were gone. I thought you were such a grown man. What is it? You didn't have anywhere to sleep tonight? No one would take you in? I guess now you're beginning to find out that life out here is no joke!"

"Robert, please, not now!" Mama's voice sounded weary.

Bobby raised his head slowly.

His mother recoiled at the sight of his tears. "Bobby?" Deep worry creased her face. She placed her hands on Bobby's face like she used to when he was a little boy. "Honey, what's the matter? You can tell me."

Bobby opened his mouth—tried to speak. But he couldn't seem to force out the words.

"It's Justin, isn't it?" she asked. "He's hurt, isn't he?"

"Yes, mama, it's Justin. LJ shot Justin, mama!"

Her hands dropped from Bobby's face. Worry was replaced by horror. "Oh God! Oh God!" She backed away from the table. "Please, Lord, don't let my baby die! Please, Lord!" Her body shook. "Where is he Bobby? Where is he?"

"He's at the club, Mama. He came down there. I told him to go home! I told him! I begged him to go home."

Her voice rose. "You left him there? That's your brother! Oh my God!"

He tried to explain. "Snake was about to shoot me. I wanted to stay, but what was I supposed to do? I ran out as fast as I could! I called 911."

Everything felt like a jumbled nightmare in his head—fragmented and surreal. He could barely make sense of it himself, let alone explain it to his panicked mother.

74

"It's all my fault," Mama wailed through tears. "I never should have let him leave the house. I knew I was feeling something bad."

Bobby's tears flowed harder. "No, it's all my fault! It's my fault! I'm sorry, Mama. I'm sorry!"

For the first time since Bobby could remember, Robert's face softened toward him. He came over and placed his hand on Bobby's shoulders. "It's okay, son. It's gonna be okay. I need to get down to that club. Emma, get my gun."

Mama's panic redoubled. "Your gun? No, Robert! You don't need a gun. We need God!"

"You bring God, I'll bring the gun. Let's go!"

By this time, Granny had come downstairs. "What dun happened? Why is everybody screaming?"

Mama sobbed. "It's Justin. Something happened to Justin."

The sound of the phone ringing nearly sent Bobby jumping out of his skin.

Mama picked it up. "Hello?"

Bobby braced himself for the worst.

"Yes, this is his mother." She turned to Robert, her eyes wide. "He's at the hospital, and he's in intensive care!" Her voice rose again. "How is he? Can't you tell me something?
Okay…okay, we're on our way." She hung up and looked at Bobby. "C'mon Bobby."

"I can't go. I've caused enough trouble."

Robert put his arm around Mama. "It's okay, Emma. Let him stay. He'll be okay. Come on, Granny. We may need your prayers after all."

They left quickly, and then there was nothing. Nothing but silence.

Alone at the kitchen table, something else began to overshadow the jumbled mess of thoughts in Bobby's mind.

Anger. Not at Robert or LJ, but at God, Himself.

He screamed into the empty kitchen. "Why? He trusted You! He never did anything wrong!"

His hands shook as he reached into one of his pockets. "I don't need You! All I need is this." He pulled out a joint, lit it up, then looked up to God. "This Bud's for you."

———————————

Sometimes I just don't know
The way that I should go
Sometimes I get so confused
Everybody, they want me to move
In the right direction
But, I got no affection
So what am I to do,
should I give in to you?
Or you Lord?
Sometimes I get so confused
In the way that I should choose
I love my mama
But I love my money

Can you tell me where to go?
In the right direction
But, I got no affection
So what am I to do
Should I give in to you?
My mama wants me to turn Thy way
But my money tells me to go on my way
All I know is what I've been told
But now I'm stuck at a fork in the road
Every one of them, it just seems so nice
Oh, but now I must sacrifice
And I got to make up my mind tonight
Can I give in? Should I give in? Can I give in to You?

He inhaled a long drag from the joint. He didn't care about anything anymore. He was just angry.

Not just about tonight. About everything. Hurts of the past reopened, fresh and raw. Why did his father have to die? Why were so many people hurting? Why were so many filled with disease? Why don't parents understand their children? Why was there so much killing in the world? Why was everyone fronting and trying to put on a phony aura of success? Why wasn't he like his brother? Why was his mother so weak?

But God remained silent.

So, he kept smoking. One joint after another.

He tried to focus on how angry he was—how much God had let him down. But one question kept popping up and wouldn't quiet: was Justin going to live?

But the pot began to do its work. With his senses dulled, a temporary relief washed over him. Bobby relaxed into it—allowed himself to be carried away.

But his peace was interrupted by the creaking of the back-door hinge that needed oiling.

Had Mama or Robert forgotten something? Before he could gather his senses, the intruder appeared in the doorway.

Snake.

There was another man Bobby didn't recognize with him. Although Bobby felt like he had seen the man before, he couldn't place him.

Snake's gun was already drawn as he started toward Bobby. Fear gripped Bobby once again. This time he knew he was done, for real. Knowing he was about to die, he turned around so that his back was to Snake and grabbed the back of his head.

The cross that dangled from his neck was now in view, and Robert's words echoed in his memory again: "One day you'll find out what that cross means."

Today was that day. Why hadn't he listened to Robert? Why hadn't he stayed in school and listened to his teachers? He wished he had gone to church and sung in the choir. He wished he had stayed home. Maybe Justin wouldn't be dead if he had.

But if Justin was dead, and Bobby was about to die, maybe he'd be able to see Justin and apologize for all the mistakes he had made. At least he hoped so.

Snake's cold voice cut into Bobby's thoughts. "You better say your prayers, church boy. Maybe your God will show you a little mercy."

Bobby felt the metal of the gun on his skull. Snake then started backing up, eerily laughing. The last thing Bobby heard was an ear-splitting bang, and then there was nothing but darkness.

"People will faint from terror, apprehensive of what is coming into the world..." Luke 21:26

Chapter 4

A Strange Place

Death was a strange place. Foggy. Dark. Bobby had no doubt that on the other side of that fog was the Hell he deserved. The scripture in the book of Psalms, chapter twenty-three, raced through his mind. He could hear his grandmother's voice: "Yea though I walk through the valley of the shadow of death, I will fear no evil, for Thou art with me."

He didn't see any fire or brimstone. There was no devil, no people running around screaming. There was no lake of fire or bottomless pit, or even cankerworms that were supposed to eat away your flesh.

Nothing.

A dark, thick, fog began to surround him like a warm, moist cloth. Bobby's head spun wildly. His mind became a tornado, blowing images across his memory. They came one by one, images of Lincoln Elementary, Belle Isle Park where he sold drugs, playing games with Justin in the backyard, and singing in the youth choir at church. A hint of nostalgia tickled his brain. There was a time when he had a lot of fun at church. The Holy Ghost had people shouting every Sunday, and his pastor could really bring the Word. Those images were whisked away when out of nowhere, a strong wind whipped around him, almost like a hurricane. He groped for something to hold on to, but there was nothing. Only fog and darkness.

The fierce wind ripped at his clothes, nearly clawing them from his body. But he didn't actually move, not even an inch.

A bright red light appeared and began circling around him. Screams of great anguish sounded like they were coming through a loudspeaker. Several spirit-like beings with no eyes or faces and with long, flowing white tendrils without any particular shape, danced strangely before his eyes.

This was it.

They were here to torment him. He'd officially arrived in Hell. Tears began to fall from his eyes. The spirits cascaded in slow motion, into the darkness, disappearing. The tears caught the eerie red light, and Bobby could see they were not tears of water, but tears of blood as they splashed on his arm.

Howling noises filled the darkness and consumed every space. What looked like a large mirror appeared before him, and his own terror was reflected back at him.

He stared at his wide, brown eyes, and the blood that streaked down his face. His mind fumbled for something that no longer seemed to be there. What was it?

His name.

Horror overwhelmed him as he realized he couldn't remember his own name. Or who he was. Or where he came from. The tornado of memories had melted away, and all that was left was vast space filled with fear.

His mind was gone. Was this what it was like to have an overdose?

A wisp of memory skittered through his brain at the thought of overdosing. Drugs. Yes, that had been a part of his lost past, hadn't it? How many people had overdosed on his product?

A drug dealer. That's who he was. Had he ever been to jail, he wondered. Is that how he had died?

His heart cried out in anguish. If only he could live again to help people instead of afflict them!

"God, please help me!"

His words appeared before him in large, white letters, furiously encircling him in a tight spiral, reverberating, echoing in the dark, then fading away.

Abruptly, tears began to flow again. Only this time, the tears weren't blood. These tears were like healing fluids traveling through an intravenous tube, giving life to those who were afflicted. It was like blood flowing back into a numb arm after sleeping on it for hours the wrong way.

His mind raced. What did it all mean?

And then, everything stopped. Only silence and darkness. He waited—counted off a full minute, but there was nothing. The minutes turned into hours. He looked down and saw the remains of some marijuana. Had he smoked that? Yes, he could just barely remember through his mental haze.

Man, I gotta leave that stuff alone!

Before another thought could cross his mind, an eerie, soft green light appeared in the dark. The fog began to lift. Still dazed and groggy, he heard what sounded like voices that seemed to come out of the dark, misty night. The voices grew louder. This was it. The nightmare was about to begin, again. The fog cleared as the voices grew louder. He blinked to clear his vision.

Yes, there, he could see something. A group of men, they seemed to be gambling.

He shook his head, rubbed his eyes, and started walking toward the group of men.

"Don't push me you stiff-necked Son of Jacob!" cried one of the men.

Bobby moved in a little closer to get a better look at the figures. The darkness seemed to slowly transition to daylight as he moved. Yes, the four men were obviously gambling, except their dice looked odd. Unfamiliar. He searched for some recollection of the dice and found none.

84

They were so different than the ones used back home. The gamblers' dice were made of wood—very large with funny-looking symbols painted on them. He cautiously walked over to the men, who didn't seem to notice him at all. They never looked up, even when he was standing right over them.

Finally, he got the nerve to speak. "What is this? Where am I?"

But they didn't respond. They kept right on gambling.

"Hey! What kind of craps y'all shootin'?"

Again, he got no answer, but then he noticed something. They were dressed in weird clothes. Weird, but familiar. He suddenly realized the clothes were like those worn long ago—in Bible days.

What kind of trick is this?

His voice came out shaky. "Okay, just tell me one thing. Why y'all dressed like that?"

Still, no word from them. They never budged and never looked his way.

Panic began to overwhelm him, again. He had not only lost his identity, but now he was sure he'd lost his mind.

But at least it wasn't Hell. Or was it?

Okay, man. Get a grip.

He scanned his surroundings, trying to figure out where he was. None of it made sense. His eyes still seemed to be adjusting to the daylight. He could make out the faint outline of some sort of buildings. Brick homes? Or was it clay or mud?

Then, seemingly out of nowhere, the whole place suddenly teemed with people dressed in ancient clothing. The ground was nothing but sand and dirt. People shouted their wares—food, clothes, other items.

A marketplace of some kind?

Goats and sheep trotted through the street. Old men with large sticks of wood they used as canes hobbled about in those same biblical clothes. Beggars clamored for money or food. It triggered a buried memory—homeless people on urban streets crying out to him as he passed by them. He knew he had never bothered to give them a dime.

A beautiful lady danced before three men. Clearly, she danced for money. Terribly familiar, yet he couldn't quite grab hold of the memory.

He forced his mind back to the present. He turned to the nearest bystander. "Where am I?"

The man kept walking.

He tried again, raising his voice. "Where are we?"

No one seemed to hear him. He tried to reach out to touch them. His hand slipped right through the arm of a passing woman. Bobby's whole body began to shake. He wasn't in Hell, but he must be dead. He had to be dead. It was the only thing.

86

The marijuana popped back into his mind. Had he overdosed on some drug laced in the weed? He wondered if there was anyone to care if he had.

Yes, there was. He could see her face in a woman—his mother. There was something else trying to break through. His mother hadn't just lost him, but also, another son.

His brother. His heart saddened again for his brother. He forced himself to temporarily wash out his thoughts.

He screamed at the people around him. "Enough is enough! Can anybody tell me what time it is?"

Nothing.

He stalked up to one person and looked the man straight in the eye. "Look man, I'm not asking for a whole lot. I'm just trying to figure out where I am. All I wanna do is get back to the crib. C'mon, somebody! I'm trying to get to my house. You know what I'm saying?"

Nothing.

He could feel the last thread of his sanity slipping away. This was like something out of a movie. Everywhere he looked, people were busy trying to survive the poor surroundings. The sand, the buildings. Something rang a bell.

The Middle East. Yes, that's where he was. He knew that now. But something was still off. The *time*. This was not his century—the twenty-first century.

Judging by the tools and utensils, this was definitely not the twenty-first century.

He plunked down in the dusty street. Details, memories, his life—it all flooded back to him. He was Bobby Bolden, a drug-dealing thug from Detroit. Tonight, he'd left his mother childless. He'd slipped into Hell, then somehow landed here—wherever here was. And he needed to try to get home, if that was possible.

He rose to his feet. "Come on somebody, I'm just trying to get back to the eastside! C'mon! Somebody gotta know something. Look, I'm gon' call it out. French Road, Conners, Gratiot, Chalmers, Mack! Dang, this ain't right God! Can anybody tell me how to get back to the eastside?" he screamed out.

Nothing.

Finally, he gave up, defeated. Clearly, no one could hear him. He could see them, but it was obvious now, they couldn't see him. He dropped back to the ground and held his head in his hands. Would he ever see his home again? He wondered if this is what the people on the streets of Detroit felt like—aimless, lost, and no one caring.

He lifted his head. The hills cut a silhouette against the sky in the distance. Another scripture his grandmother used to quote came to mind: "Look to the hills from which comes your help, your help comes from the Lord."

88

Bobby began to sob. "God, please get me home. Please tell me how to get back. I promise, Lord, no more smoking! I'm sorry, Lord."

"Psst," an intruding voice cut into his cries. "Psst." At first he couldn't tell where it came from. Bobby looked around, but he didn't see anything. "Psst, over here," the voice came again.

Bobby glanced over his shoulder. About twenty feet away stood a man dressed like he was from the 'hood. He wore a vintage California Angel's snapback baseball cap, a pair of Levi's, and a baseball shirt that read, Angels. He looked like he hadn't missed any meals lately, weighing in at least at 270 pounds. He motioned for Bobby to come over to him.

Bobby hesitated, then obeyed.

The man smiled. "Turn right on Cadieux Road, then left on Warren, and take that all the way to Van Dyke." He strode away without another word.

Bobby stood in stunned silence for a moment. But then he took off after him. He caught up to the man and grabbed him by his arm. Apparently, he could touch this guy, unlike the others. "Hold up! Hold up! You can hear me? I can touch you!"

The man just stared blankly.

"You can hear me!" Bobby whooped aloud again. "You aren't going anywhere. Oh my God, you can hear me! Thank you, Jesus!" The man frowned and tried to pull away.

But Bobby gripped harder. "You aren't going anywhere. Oh my God, you can hear me, and I can feel you!" He could barely contain his excitement.

The man struggled. "Yes, I can hear you! You don't have to scream in my ear!" He pulled against Bobby's grip. "What are you doing, man? All you dudes from Detroit are the same. Everything going good, we don't hear anything from you. You just dancing and partying and having a good time. But as soon as you get into a little bit of trouble, it's 'Father, Jesus, help me somebody'! Next thing you know, I'm on assignment again!"

Bobby looked at him, bewildered. "Wait, wait, hold up. I need two things from you. First of all, where am I? And secondly, how come you can hear me and the rest of these people are acting like 'Children of The Corn'?"

The man frowned again. "Well, to answer your first question, if I have my bearings correct, we are in Nazareth, Galilee, about 1 B.C., and Herod is king."

"Nazareth? That ain't on the eastside!"

The man rolled his eyes. "No, it's not. You're a bright one, aren't you? Now, before I answer your second question, did you ever go to Vacation Bible School?"

90

Before Bobby could answer, the man continued. "Didn't think so. What about Sunday school?"

Again, as the words were coming off of Bobby's lips, the man interrupted. "Hmm … didn't do that either. If you read the Bible, it lets you know that every one of God's children—good and bad, every color—*everybody* has an angel watching over them. Now, because of some things that went down in the heavenly realms—none of your business, don't ask—I got the best assignment on earth. I am your guardian angel." He looked up at the sky, one eyebrow raised and sarcastically muttered, "Thanks a lot Father. Really appreciate it!"

Bobby looked the man up and down. "You don't look like an angel to me. Where are your wings?"

The man ignored him. "Listen, before you start asking a whole bunch of questions, I need to get some things straight with you. There are only a few things you need to know. I'm not a genie, so you don't get three wishes. There are certain things I can do for you, and there are other things I have no control over because it's already written in the logbook."

That's it. I've officially gone off the deep-end.

Maybe it was the drugs, or the stress of his brother being shot. But Nazareth, 1 B.C., an angel who looks like a huge Chris Rock, and people that he could see, who couldn't see him? Nothing made sense.

Bobby tried to sort through what the angel had told him. "So, what's this business about a logbook? You keeping tabs on me?"

"The Logbook. It's the Word, the Scriptures, the Bible. Get it?"

"Hold on, hold up. You're really trying to tell me I have a guardian angel?"

"I told you that already," the angel snapped.

"But look at you. Look how you're dressed. You don't look biblical to me."

"Let me tell you something, son. Do you see these people? You don't want me to open their eyes. If they could see you dressed all crazy with your pants hanging off your butt, tattoos all over your arms, and an earring in your ear, they would take you outside the city walls and have you stoned. Trying to look like Lil' Wayne or Drake. Talking about, 'Whoa, I'm up in Nazareth!', please!"

Bobby stared at him. "Hold up, I'm getting this now. You watch BET …?"

The angel glared at Bobby. "Yeah, we see everything you do. Every time you picked up a crack pipe, I saw you. Every time you smoked a blunt, I saw you. Every time you let curse words flow from your lips, I heard you. Every time you disrespected your parents, I saw you. Every dime bag you sold to those kids, I saw you."

Bobby's mouth dropped open. "Excuse me?"

But the angel snorted back, "Excuse me?" then started singing. "Every breath you take, every move you make, I've been watching you." Then he reached into his pocket and pulled out a shiny object. "And another thing: I'm getting a little too old to be catching bullets." Bobby stared at the bullet. With a jolt, he realized he recognized this man—he was the same man who had come in with Snake.

This man had stopped the bullet.

But rebellion flared inside Bobby, anyway. He backed away from the angel. "Hold up, God. He's getting a little too personal for me. He don't know me!" Looking at his angel, he shouted, "You don't know me! You don't know nothing about me. You're no angel! You're the devil! Get me up out of here!"

"Be careful my brother, that sounds like blasphemy."

Bobby fell to his knees. "Please God, please, just get me back. I don't belong here!"

The angel walked right past him without a backwards glance. "Chill out, dude. I've got business to take care of here."

He marched into one of the houses. Bobby watched warily for a moment, but then jogged to catch up. It wasn't like he had anywhere else to go.

Inside, he saw a young woman, maybe fifteen, maybe a bit older. Her face, though not glamorous, was beautiful in its own way. It seemed to glow. Bobby knew she was special. He could feel it. He knew this was a special moment.

In the time of my Savior's life
He came forth as a gentle Christ
But men couldn't see just who He was
He came to us for a worthy cause
In the day that the world was lost
He came forth just to bear the cross
To redeem mankind from sinful shame
To make all men to know His name
Jesus ... The Son of God
The Lamb of God
The Mighty Lord!

The angel spoke to the young girl. She didn't seem to be able to see the angel, though Bobby still could. The angel's voice sounded different from when he spoke to Bobby. This time, he spoke with more authority. And he sounded...divine. This time, he sounded like an angel—or at least what Bobby thought an angel should sound like. Slowly the angel came into the young girl's view, and she was frightened.

"Hail!" the angel's voice rang out.

With that one word, she fell to her knees. The room dimmed, and all Bobby could see was a serene, white light pouring down from the corner of the ceiling.

He couldn't see the angel clearly anymore. There was only the white light.

But he could still hear the angel's voice. "You, who are highly favored, the Lord is with you; blessed are you among women."

The young girl trembled on the floor. "Who are you? And what are you saying to me?"

"Fear not, stand on your feet, for you will conceive a child in your womb and will bring forth a son. And you will call his name...Jesus. He will be great and will be called The Son of The Highest, and the Lord God will give unto him the throne of his father David, and he will reign in the house of Jacob forever, and of his kingdom there will be no end."

Bobby realized this had to be Mary, the mother of Jesus. She looked so young. He hadn't thought of Mary being a teenager. She was also taller than he imagined and average-looking—not like the pictures he saw at church or in a Bible. It was no question she was poor. Her house only contained the bare necessities—a couple of old chairs, a table, and a cot that must have been her bed. Bobby began to think about the things in his house back home. He knew he was blessed when he compared his home with Mary's. Here, there was no running water, no electricity, no family room with a big flat-screen television, and certainly no beautiful backyard with a small basketball court. An odd thought struck him.

I appreciate all the things Robert has provided for my family—and I can't believe I'm saying it. The moment was surreal, to say the least. Bobby almost felt like an intruder, like he didn't belong there, yet he knew there was some purpose for him, something he had to learn.

The young, virgin girl interrupted his thoughts, "How shall this be, seeing I know not a man?"

The angel answered her, his voice strong but reassuring. "The Holy Ghost will come upon you, and the power of the Highest will overshadow you. Therefore, also that holy thing which is born in you, will be called the Son of God. Know this, your cousin Elizabeth, has also conceived a son in her old age."

And with that, the voice faded and so did the angel. Bobby looked everywhere, but the angel had gone.

Mary spoke again. "Behold the maidservant of the Lord. Let it be unto me according to your word. I must go to Judea to share my joy with Elizabeth—she will be excited, but will she believe that I've never known a man?"

Bobby snorted. "You can forget that."

Mary dashed from the house. Bobby's angel was gone. He had no choice but to follow Mary. She walked for what seemed like miles. After a while, Mary's breathing became heavy and she seemed to be slowing down.

Weird. I'm not tired at all.

Finally, they reached a house and Mary stopped to knock on an old-looking front door. A woman answered. Her drab, simple dress pulled tightly across a swollen belly. Elizabeth, Mary's cousin the angel had spoken of.

"Grace and peace, Elizabeth," Mary greeted her cousin. Elizabeth grabbed her own stomach because the child in her suddenly moved.

A grin crept across Elizabeth's face. She reached out and touched Mary's stomach. "Blessed are you among women and blessed is the fruit of your womb. You must believe all that was spoken to you."

Bobby slumped in a corner of the small front room of Elizabeth's house. He was an outsider again, a witness to events he didn't understand and certainly wasn't a part of.

Mary smiled, joy illuminating her features. "My soul magnifies the Lord and my spirit rejoices in God, my Savior."

———————

My soul doth magnify the Lord
My spirit has rejoiced in Him
He is great and marvelous
And holy is
Holy is His name
And holy is
Holy is His name
Blessed be for He has chosen me

97

Hallelujah!
Blessed be for He has blessed you too
Hallelujah!
Worthy is He
Lord of Israel
He shall be great
His name Emmanuel
And His mercy is on them
That fear Him
He has done great things
With His mighty arm
Magnify His holy name
Magnify His holy name!
Hallelujah!

Blessed are thou among women
And blessed is the fruit of thy womb
For as soon as I heard thy voice
The life down in my soul
Leaped for joy
And blessed is she that believes
My soul doth magnify the Lord
And my spirit has rejoiced
In God my Savior
For He that is mighty
Has done to me great things
And holy is His name
And His mercy is on them that fear Him
He has shown great strength

> *With his mighty hand*
> *He has filled the hungry*
> *And the rich he sent away*
> *Blessed be the Lord God of Israel*
> *For He has redeemed His people*
> *And He has raised up the horn of Salvation*
> *Magnify ... magnify His holy name!*

———————————

Mary's sweet voice carried through the room as she continued to rejoice. "For He that is mighty has done to me great things, and Holy is His name."

Bobby rolled his eyes. Just a bunch of religious talk, like at church. A moment later, commotion in the street outside began to drown out Mary's words.

Bobby rose and peered out of the door. Roman soldiers marched through the dusty streets, and trumpets blared. A huge crowd had gathered in a frenzy. Bobby could almost taste their fear as they huddled together in clusters and shied away from the soldiers. One of the soldiers barked out his orders. He looked tougher than Snake or any of the other guys in Bobby's 'hood.

"To all the citizens of the land, it is hereby decreed by the Emperor of Rome, Caesar Augustus, that a census be taken throughout the empire. Every person is required to return to his ancestral home for registration. Any who defy this order shall stand before the governor who will determine their fate, and death shall be your likely outcome!"

The glare punctuating his orders seemed to sum up the relationship between the people and the Roman government.

Bobby's angel stood in the street as if he was waiting for him. Everyone else dispersed just as quickly as they came. The angel went in the opposite direction of the people. Bobby watched him walk away, but this time he realized he'd better follow if he had any hope of getting out of this place.

"Hey, Angel, wait for me!"

Chapter 5

An Evil Plan

Bobby held onto his angel like a little boy holding onto his daddy's shirt. He couldn't feel the ground under his feet. "Are we walking on clouds?"

The angel ignored him and kept moving.

Fine, then. I'll simply hold you tighter, maybe then you'll say something.

Wherever they were headed, it was kind of cool riding with an angel, but fear also was foaming in Bobby's gut. Thoughts flashed through his mind. Where was he? What was happening to him? *Why* was it happening? There were so many questions.

He glanced at Angel. It was the only name he could think to call his companion and guide. New respect for this being was beginning to grow. He sensed Angel had the answers—and knew why Bobby felt there was something great he was still supposed to witness.

Suddenly, incense and strange perfumes filled the air. A flurry of beautiful colors enveloped them—red, purple, and gold tapestry, the sort Bobby had never seen before. He was totally mystified and totally in awe at what he was seeing.

Bobby and Angel walked through a maze of colorful corridors where even the door handles sparkled gold. Angel entered through an archway, and Bobby scrambled to follow. Pristine, white statues of Roman kings flanked the walls of the room. The ceiling was draped with all manner of fine cloth. Everything seemed to glitter.

A room fit for a king. Opulence.

Bobby's eyes scanned the room, and then stopped on a man who sat on a large throne studded with all sorts of precious stones. His gray beard ended with a full complement of carefully guided curls. The garment he wore was obviously very expensive, lined and stitched in what appeared to be gold. Beneath him and all around him, beautiful women clad in gold and silver garments, stretched out like lounging housecats alongside men who obviously had a little too much to drink.

A woman stood to the side of the man on the throne. She held a fan of blue-green peacock feathers and slowly fanned the seated man in the uncomfortable heat. The man snored and shifted in his sleep.

Long night of partying, I guess.

This sleeping figure in gold could only be a king.

He began twitching on his throne and growled deep in his throat. He seemed to be having a nightmare of some sort.

Yeah, welcome to my world.

Angel nodded to the side of the throne, as if he wanted Bobby to sit down. Bobby shot him a look and whispered, "Seriously?"

"Sit."

Bobby sat, eyeing the man on the throne warily. The man snorted again, he jerked side to side, his nightmare intensifying. Then he started to awaken. He let out a loud scream, then quickly gathered his composure. He grumbled to himself. "Silly me. It was only a dream." His voice turned into a high-pitched shrill as he shouted, "I am king! I should not be subject to rumors and speculation!"

Crazy.

The woman with the fan temporarily slowed her pace and raised an eyebrow.

"Rumors!" The king's words slurred. He slammed his fist to the arm of his throne and nearly toppled over. "Some dare to say there is a new king in the land? I am first in my line, and I will rule with my word, I will rule with my wine." He paused to hiccup. "And I will rule with my sword!"

The king cackled, and the sound of it sent chills through Bobby.

The king pointed a finger at one of the lounging women. "If anyone, and I do mean anyone, even so much as think that he or she, shall rise up against me, him I shall destroy!" He pushed his bulk to his feet, then strolled around like a lion stalking his prey.

He rambled loudly and seemed to be talking to himself. "Why? Why? Because killing is like eating. It's something that simply must be done. My appetite grows increasingly acute with these troublemakers."

He laughed and plunked back down into his seat. "More wine!"

Bobby stared at him. What was wrong with this guy?

A nut cake, like the crackheads back in the 'hood, I guess.

But it still didn't answer Bobby's most nagging question. Why had Angel brought him here?

One of the women gingerly approached the king. "But, O King, your greatness has been measured by your own wisdom, and by this great kingdom, not by the blood of these people. We only make heroes of their dead, and others will simply rise up. Why all the killing?"

The king moved in a flash, despite his drunken state. He grabbed her arm while fire raged in his eyes. "Why? Because I am king!" He threw her to the floor with a thud.

Whoa!

104

Bobby resisted the urge to help the woman up. There was no shame in this king's game.

Just like Mike, shamefully throwing women around because of his superior strength. Mike made a habit of being rough with the ladies, and even worse than that, it seemed that many women back home enjoyed the men who were meanest to them.

It never really mattered to Bobby before, but now it was clear that those women were blind to what was really best for them. Could it be that he and his friends were blind too, mimicking what they saw on TV?

The king's shout cut through Bobby's thoughts. "I was king yesterday, and I am certainly king today. I'll be king tomorrow, and I, yes I, will be king forever!" He snapped his fingers and a stone-faced guard appeared. "Summon my royal cupbearer at once. I need more wine." Then he ascended the golden stairs of his dais and settled into his throne.

A moment later, another soldier entered the room with a man who looked like an old sage or a man of wisdom.

"Ah, it is one of the scribes. Welcome. Have some wine, or perhaps one of my harlots. I have plenty, you know." The king smiled and gestured to the women scattered all over the room.

The old man said nothing. Perhaps he was only there to make the king look official.

"O King of Judea, I have an inquiry for you," the soldier announced.

"Hold your peace!" shouted the king. Then he swallowed a large gulp of wine. After clearing his throat, he bellowed, "Now you may speak."

"There are wise men—astrologers from across the Eastern lands—asking about the newborn king of the Jews."

The king flung his robe aside and snarled. "Newborn king? Was I was born yesterday... or today?" He approached another soldier and leaned into the man's face. "Do I look like a baby?"

The soldier didn't respond, but Bobby saw the soldier's Adam's apple bob as he swallowed.

The soldier stepped forward and cleared his throat. "If you will permit, I will inquire of the guard, O King."

The king slowly moved toward the soldier, examining him closely. Then he scoffed. "If you will permit, I will inquire of the guard, O King. You must be new here?"

The soldier bowed. "My apologies, my lord."

The king laughed and motioned for more wine. "My wine! Bring me more wine! I feel good. Let us celebrate, for I am still king! Let us dance!"

The people were slow to move at first, some still struggling to wake up.

The king roared, "I said dance!"

Musicians seemed to appear out from the walls and began playing their stringed instruments.

The scantily clad women danced sensually to the music. Bobby was smacked with a feeling of déjà vu. Wasn't this just like the club back home with LJ and his homies? Didn't they fling dollar bills at dancing girls just like this?

He turned to Angel. "Who is this king?"

"His name is Herod."

The extra wine had a jovial effect on King Herod. He leered at the women, toying and dancing with them as he continued to drink. A soldier approached him and whispered in his ear. Herod nodded, and the soldier motioned to have certain wise men brought in. They began to show the king some kind of document—a scroll of some sort.

Bobby's curiosity ate at him. Finally, he leaned over to Angel. "What are those men showing him?"

"They're showing him the ancient words of the prophets. They're showing him that there will be a child born of a virgin, who will rise and become king over all of Israel."

Herod's scream shattered the atmosphere. "Out! Out! Everyone out of my sight!"

No problem, man!

Bobby wanted to leave but resisted his urge to run out. Those around him scrambled towards the door but seemed careful not to turn their backs to Herod.

They all bowed away backwards and quickly scattered into the lateness of the night.

Herod shouted again to the chief soldier. Bobby assumed he was the chief soldier, since his helmet was arrayed in a scarlet, feathered décor. "Soldier, ready the men for battle, for tonight we shall march upon these stiff-necked people!"

Herod strolled up to his throne. "I am forever King of the Jews! Rumors, lies, stupidity, and slander! I don't need wise men. I don't need scribes and astrologers. I am sure these men have come to mock me, and now my wrath is stirred. Prophecies, bah! Lies! All lies! Since these stupid commoners believe so highly in their sacred scrolls, out of them I shall fulfill their own word. In Ramah there was a voice heard, lamentation, and weeping and great mourning. Rachel weeping for her dead children." He laughed. "Yes! Yes!"

Bobby moved away from the madman. He sounded like he was possessed by an evil spirit. The king's hands trembled and his eyes were bloodshot.

The veins in his neck protruded as he raised his voice again. "I shall slay all the children two years and under until the city weeps and the streets run red with their blood!"

Bobby turned to Angel. "You're not going to let him do it, are you? You are going to stop him, aren't you?"

108

Angel said nothing.

Bobby tried again, as if trying to make up for his error with Justin. He was not about to let something bad happen again. "Well, if you don't do anything, I will. I'll warn the people!"

He tried to leave, but Angel held him back.

Herod was storming about the room again. He stopped before his commander. "Soldier! What say ye?"

"O King, the men are prepared for battle."

"Good, good. Then let me remind you, fulfill the prophecy as I have ordered. Spare the women, for they must weep. But spare the children and I shall personally cast your head in a river from the tip of my sword! Do you understand my orders?"

The soldier bowed. "Orders heard, orders received, orders given!"

With a flourish of his hand, Herod called out, "Then with your swiftest horses and your strongest men, we shall have the victory! What are you waiting for? Sound the trumpet and let the march begin!"

Trumpets blared and soldiers from every corner of the room lined up in formation. Then they began their death march out of the palace.

Bobby broke away from Angel. He sprinted from the room and into the city streets as fast as he could.

When Herod realized that he had been outwitted by the Magi, he was furious, and he gave orders to kill all the boys...Matt. 2:16

Chapter 6

Surrounded by Death

When Bobby got to the marketplace, the unsuspecting mothers were quietly doing their chores. Children were running around, playing a game that reminded Bobby of tag.

He yelled out to them. "Hey!" The word was nearly lost in his gasps for breath. Somehow, this time he felt tired, unlike before. "Herod's coming to kill your kids! You gotta get out of here! You gotta run!"

No one heard him.

Bobby gripped his head with both hands, helplessness washing over him. "Can anybody hear me? Please, you gotta to hear me!"

He looked up and saw Angel about twenty yards away, a blank expression on his face.

Bobby ran to Angel. "Look, you can't let this happen. Don't you understand? You can't let them kill these children. They're innocent—they're just babies!"

Angel stared at his distraught fugitive from a distant world. Sympathy glistened in Angel's eyes, but there was resignation there, too. He wanted to help but the event was already written in the logbook, or whatever he called it.

Finally, he spoke. "You see, Bobby, the enemy's been at work for a long time. He's killing kids here, and he's killing kids back in your neighborhood. Drive-by shootings, kids selling drugs and being shot, HIV…he doesn't care. He hasn't changed the way he works. He's destroying neighborhoods, families are being torn apart, young men are going to jail in record numbers while young women are being abused every day. He's all about sex, money, and sittin' high. But it's a short life, Bobby. It's a dead-end road. All that glitters isn't gold."

Bobby knew he was right. It was the same thing he had heard many times before, just in a different setting. Greed, and the desire for power pushed people to act reckless and uncaring. Selfish people lorded their power over the weak. People who thought they were gods deceived others at any cost. People were possessed by evil spirits; their hearts were full of hate and envy.

These were the authorities that ruled Bobby's world, and the young religiously followed them. Understanding his world finally began to spread through his mind. He began to see how much he was influenced by what he saw on TV and what he heard in the music he listened to. He did what the music and the many videos he watched suggested because it made him feel like he was in touch with the happenings. He wore his pants sagging because his idols did. He used

112

profanity and disrespected his parents and teachers because the 'authorities' in his world did.

He didn't go to church because it wasn't the cool thing to do. He now realized that he was being used—suckered into a world of deception and illusions. And it was only the beginning of what was to come.

Bobby's reflections of the world he knew was interrupted by what sounded like thunder in the distance. He looked up at the sky but saw no gray clouds. The thunder boomed louder and louder. Then he understood—it was the sound of horse's hooves filling the air, soldiers on a desperate mission in search of a baby king whom Herod had never seen.

Bobby's heart pounded in his chest like it had when he was at the club facing off with LJ. For a moment, he thought about his brother. Tears began to well up in his eyes. A cloud of grief threatened to swallow him.

I'm sorry, Justin.

Shouted warnings snapped Bobby back to the dusty streets of Judea.

"The soldiers are coming! The soldiers are coming!"

Bobby raised his voice and joined the cried warnings. But no matter what he did, he couldn't make them hear him.

By now he was completely exasperated, but he couldn't stop. He reached for the shoulder of a young mother holding an infant.

113

"Hey lady, you got to leave. Herod's coming to kill your kids!" But Bobby's hand slipped right through the woman's shoulder.

Angel stood about fifty yards away. "I'm sorry, Bobby. They can't hear you."

Bobby did a double-take. Though Angel was far away, he could still hear his voice, almost crystal clear.

He ran toward Angel and grabbed his shirt. He felt the soft fabric of the shirt, soft as anything he ever felt. Strange how he could touch Angel but not the others. "Angel, they gotta hear me!"

"I'm sorry, Bobby. It's no use. They can't hear you."

"Then they'll hear you! You've got to help them!"

"I'm sorry, Bobby. It's in the logbook. There's nothing I can do."

The soldiers had now stormed into the marketplace and surrounded the mothers and children. The terror on the mother's faces told it all. They had seen death from these murderous intruders before. They knew they were the unwanted, the minority, the lower class, and the unloved in a society of devils. The women clutched onto their children even tighter, hiding the sweet faces from the power-drunk agents of death.

A commanding soldier bellowed, "By orders of King Herod, all the boys two years and under must be slain, leave not one alive! Kill them all!"

With that, the soldiers tore the young boys away from their mother's arms. Blood spilled in every direction. Children screamed. Other older children ran in haste ahead of the soldiers through the village, desperate for escape. Mothers wailed in the streets. It reminded Bobby of terrorist attacks that bring death and grief to people all over the world. Like the senseless animals of his day, these murderous sub-human beings showed no mercy. To him, they were just like the dealers who ravaged neighborhoods back home. He felt bad now that he realized he was part of that evil activity.

Bobby had never experienced such pain before. He felt utterly helpless. Again, he looked at the cross dangling from his neck and Robert's words came screaming again: "One day, you'll know what that cross stands for."

He tried to rip it off his neck but it wouldn't break. No matter how hard he tried, it wasn't going anywhere. Where was God now, when he needed Him? Where were the men—the husbands and fathers—in this city of death?

It seemed that the bloodshed would never end. But finally, the screams quieted and only sobbing remained.

The commanding officer shouted to one of his subordinates. "Is it done?"

"Yes, it is finished!"

"All of them? Are all the boys dead?"

115

"Yes, we have destroyed them all."

A young boy's cry cut through the chorus of weeping mothers. A mother with a young toddler in her arms, darted from behind one of the clay and mud houses and took off down the street. She stumbled once but clung fast to the boy as she regained her footing.

The commanding officer whistled, and another soldier caught up to the woman in a flash. One blow from his fist, sent her toppling into the dust-filled street. Blood spilled from her nose and mouth.

Anger rose inside Bobby. "Stop!"

And then the world slowed, everything moving in slow motion. Robert came to mind again. How could Robert hit Bobby's mother then turn around and talk about the cross? The thought made him want to explode.

His mind began to spin out of control. He thought about helpless children being sexually and physically abused by adults. He thought about homeless people sleeping on rain-soaked sidewalks with nothing to eat. He thought about LJ using him and other teenagers to sell the insidious drugs that tore up the neighborhoods of Detroit. He thought about crooked cops who allowed it all to occur, just to get their share of the money. His stomach roiled. It was disgusting— and certainly not of God.

He thought of many of his friends.

These were people he knew who had lost their lives to gunfire in a crack house over a measly fifty bucks. He thought of all the clubs on 8mile Rd., where thousands of dollars were spent every night, giving young girls the false hope of the good life. He thought of Mike and other young ballers trying to make a name for themselves. The world was sick, and people in high places were allowing it to be so.

If I were in one of those high places, I would change things.

The world around him had created so many false illusions. That's why he and his friends were in trouble. Thousands of young men and women were in prison because of the illusions they embraced.

These are the same illusions that had killed many in the generations before him. Now they were killing his generation. It was like his eyes had opened for the first time, and he saw right through the illusions of sex, explicit music, designer clothing, apathetic and cold attitudes, and the love of money. It all made sense to him now. These things were designed to control his mind—to take from him whatever he had, all the while, making others rich. They were designed to destroy his soul and his future.

And he had bought into it.

The world around Bobby sped up again. A desperate and helpless mother lay in the street, knocked out, and her little boy, dazed when his mother fell,

117

toddled away. A nearby soldier, quickly scooped him up.

The commanding officer's voice boomed. "Bring him to me! He must be the one the king spoke of."

The boy's mother, finally gaining her senses, struggled to get to her knees. Then she wobbled onto her feet, "My baby! Not my baby! Please don't do it!"

The commanding officer pounded her to the ground again. "Yes, this has to be the one. Soldier, give him to me. Hurry! We'll make quick work of him for the king."

The little boy's eyes bulged out. He lay pinned under the weight of the soldier's knee. The officer lifted his sword high and brought it down swiftly into the child's chest.

Bobby turned away, but he was a second too late. The image burned in his mind. Had he really just witnessed that awful event?

A heart-rending scream drew Bobby's attention back to the little boy who just lost his life in this horrific massacre. The boy's mother lay slumped in the dirt, crying from the depths of her being. This time it wasn't guns and AR 15's like in Bobby's day, it was swords and knives, but the result was still the same. People lost their lives over foolishness due to the deranged mental state of so many.

118

The commanding officer held the boy's lifeless body before the cowering masses. "Is this your king? Do you bow before this king or Herod the Great?"

Then he placed the boy into the arms of his brokenhearted mother.

The officer stepped around the still bodies and grieving mothers. He nodded to one of his soldiers. "Tell the king that Rachel weeps indeed."

Bobby's rage boiled over. He ran toward the soldier, but the man seemed out of his reach now, disappearing into the mist.

Still, Bobby shouted at the top of his voice. "How could you do this? They were only children! They were only children! Why?" He tried to curse, but the words were halted in his mouth by some strange force he had never felt before.

Instead, he fell to his knees and sobbed. "Why?"

He was my only child
You should have seen His smile
He never did anything
To deserve this death
Can somebody tell me why?
He was my only Son
He was my only One
My baby brought Joy
To my day

119

As I watched him grow up and play
I can't understand
I will never see my baby become a man
Now there's grief and trouble all over the land
Can you tell me why?
There's so much killing all over this land
Mothers against daughters
Sons against fathers
Race against race

Defeated, Bobby slumped into the blood-stained street. He could feel evil smoldering from the village, echoing the hell that had arisen from below. He cried with the others.

After a few moments, someone approached Bobby. He could just make him out through the blur of tears in his eyes. There was something Bobby couldn't help but notice—the bronze color of his feet. When he tried to look up to see who the man was, all he saw was red. Red, everywhere. There was so much blood, he couldn't seem to see anything else.

The man with feet colored bronze, stooped down, took the bottom of his robe, and wiped the tears from Bobby's eyes. "Blessed is the man that walks not in the plans of the ungodly, nor sits among those who are scornful and evil, but his delight is in the law of God. God will never leave him nor forsake him."

The man rose, then strolled away.

Bobby stared after him. Even in the midst of death and sorrow, the man's words brought calm to his heart—a calm he had never felt before. It was the kind of peace that he heard his grandmother talk about from time to time. He remembered her words well, "There's a peace that passes all understanding." Bobby also remembered how he had heard that same scripture from his pastor. He never gave it much thought, but now the meaning of it was so clear.

"And I, if I be lifted up from the earth, will draw all men unto me..."
John 12:32

Chapter 7

Choosing Life

It seemed to Bobby as though he had been asleep for weeks. The tears that soaked his shirt had dried. Although his brain seemed wrapped in fog, there was at least one thing clear in his mind—the fear of opening his eyes and not being at home.

The only way he could get home was to awaken from this crazy dream. But how?

When I open my eyes, I'll be back in my living room, on the floor. This nightmare will be over.

Bobby repeated it over and over to himself. Snake never came in. There was no gun. Justin hadn't been shot. There was no Angel. Bobby had simply passed out from smoking too much weed, which could have been laced with another drug.

He tried to open his eyes, but he couldn't force himself to do it. He listened to the sounds around him. He heard the sounds of people milling about, engulfed in small talk. Excitement was buzzing through the air.

He tried hard to ignore the noise, which unfortunately for him, was not coming from his own living room, although he hoped it was.

When I open my eyes, I'll be back where I belong. Back in the D. Back on the eastside. Finally, he pried his eyes open. The man with the bronze feet was in his view and stood before him. His hair looked like wool, and there seem to be a glow that surrounded him. Bobby couldn't look directly into His face. The man stood in the midst of hundreds of people, many of whom were crippled, blind, or ailing in some way. Bobby huffed out a sigh of disappointment. He was still stuck in this strange place.

Images of the murdered children kept popping into his mind. Innocent blood, spilling into the streets. He thought of the blood spilled on the streets of Detroit—his friends who had died from gunshot wounds, drive-by shootings, and overdosing. The sound of mothers screaming at funerals echoed through his memory.

But somehow, through all of that darkness, as he looked at the figure of this man who was obviously divine, he could feel a sense of peace—a sense of hope.

Then the man spoke.

"If any man thirst, let him come unto me, and drink. He that believes on me, as the Scripture has said, out of his belly shall flow rivers of living water."

Bobby didn't know what to think. He looked again at the bronze-colored feet of the man and the strange glow that surrounded him. It had to be the same man who wiped the tears from his eyes.

124

A woman from the crowd called out, "Of a truth, this man is the Prophet."

Still another said, "Is Christ coming out of Galilee?"

"I know…He is the Christ!" someone else declared.

"Yes! Didn't the scriptures say that the Christ would come out of the seed of David and out of the town of Bethlehem, where David was born?"

"This must be Jesus," Bobby whispered to himself. "Is it really Him? It has to be. Who else could he be?"

As Bobby watched and listened to Him, the message finally started to sink into his heart. He began to feel like there really was a God who loved him. His new sense of understanding forced him to pull away from Jesus, recognizing he had no right to be in His presence. Every sin he had ever committed rushed to his head and pursed on his lips, momentarily stunning him with shame and grief.

"I shouldn't be here. I'm not worthy."

He was thinking out loud, and although the people couldn't hear him, Angel, who was back on the scene, motioned to him to be quiet, maybe just out of divine respect.

Another commotion arose just behind Bobby. Men dressed in religious garb strode to the front of the crowd.

They looked like what Bobby would consider middle-class, not rich, but certainly not poor. In their clutches was a woman dressed in black with a veil covering her face. Even though the veil shrouded her face, Bobby could feel fear radiating from her. The religious men brought the woman near Jesus and shoved her to the ground.

Again, Bobby had the urge to help, but he knew better this time. He finally understood there was nothing he could do. He finally understood that even if he never got back home, there were things that God wanted him to see.

But he frowned at the people who *were* there— those standing around Jesus and the woman. How could they stand there and watch the woman being abused? It was like the people back home who would stand around and watch a helpless victim of gang violence being beaten and violated—people who wouldn't even give the police a description of the perpetrators. So many people stand by and watch violence happen, afraid to get involved, afraid of being a victim themselves.

Bobby's thoughts were interrupted when one of the religious men stepped forward and began to speak to Jesus. His tone was one of condemnation. "Master, this woman was caught in the very act of adultery. Now the Law of Moses has commanded that she should be stoned. But what do you say?" His eyes glittered with challenge.

Memories of Sunday school lessons slowly came into focus. Bobby knew who these religious men were—Pharisees, enemies of Jesus. And they were trying to trap Him.

But Jesus didn't answer the Pharisee. Instead, He kneeled to the ground and began to write in the dust with his finger, almost as if He hadn't heard the man.

The other Pharisee lifted his nose in the air. "Master, did you not hear what we said? This woman has sinned against the Law of Moses. She has committed adultery. We saw her with our own eyes. She should be put to death! But what do you say?"

Jesus stood up. To Bobby, He seemed taller now. His voice carried authority, yet it was soft, somehow—sensitive and sincere, pulling you in and making you listen more closely. "Whoever among you is without sin, let that man first cast a stone at her."

One by one, the people started to turn away. Some glanced down at the woman as they passed her by. No one said a word. Before long, except for a few, they were all gone, including the Pharisees.

Bobby turned to Angel. "Man, this happens every day in my 'hood. Sleeping around ain't no big deal. Everybody does it."

Angel looked at him, and the scene around them seemed to freeze for a moment. "Is AIDS a big deal?"

Bobby clamped his mouth shut.

Jesus knelt beside the woman, who was still lying on the ground peeking through her veil. "Woman, where are your accusers? Didn't even one of them condemn you?"

"No sir, not even one." Her voice trembled. She stared at Him in awe.

Bobby thought his face must look the same as the woman's, wide-eyed and open-mouthed.

Jesus helped the woman up. "And neither do I. Go, and sin no more."

Those that were still there realized that this was no ordinary man. He spoke with authority and yet with compassion.

Then Jesus began to reveal more about himself to them. As He spoke, more and more people seemed to come from nowhere to hear Him.

"I am the Light of the world. He that follows me shall not walk in darkness but shall have the light of life. Truly, truly, I say to you, I am the door of the sheep. The thief comes to steal, and to kill, and to destroy. But I am come that you might have life, and that you might have it more abundantly."

While Jesus spoke, He began to heal people from all sorts of diseases. He opened a blind man's eyes. He made a lame man walk again. He caused a deaf woman to hear. The crowd gasped. People whispered. Many kissed His feet and worshipped Him. Afterward, He turned to a few men who were following

128

Him and His teachings. "Come, let us go again into Judea."

It was at that moment Bobby began to feel he needed to follow Him, too. So, he rose to his feet, dusted himself off, as if that would make him more presentable. He wanted the Man whose face seemed to have no specific color, to say something to him. He wanted Him to recognize he was there, right next to Him. But He never looked at him.

One of the disciples said, "Master, the Jews wanted to stone you the last time we were in Judea. Why would you go there again?"

"Are there not twelve hours in a day?" Jesus asked. "If a man walks in the day, he doesn't stumble because he sees the light of the world. But if a man walks in the dark, he stumbles because there is no light in him. Our friend Lazarus is dead, but I go that I may awake him out of his sleep."

But the disciple didn't seem to want to let it go. "But Lord, if Lazarus is dead, then he does well. There is nothing we can do."

Bobby remembered the preaching of his former pastor, preaching about a man named Lazarus. He turned to Angel. "Hey, so He is the Man that—"

"Shh. You're talking too much."

His disciples leaned in as though they were anticipating another revelation. Jesus began to teach his disciples again. "Lazarus is dead. But I am glad for your sakes that I was not there, to the intent you may believe. Nevertheless, come, let us go to him."

When they came near to where Lazarus lived, a woman burst through the crowd. She fell at the feet of Jesus, weeping.

"Lord, Lord, if you had been here, my brother would not have died, but I know, that even now, whatever you will ask of God, God will give it to you." Desperation creased her brow.

Jesus lifted her gently. His voice was filled with compassion. "Your brother shall rise again."

But instead of taking heart, the woman looked defeated and frustrated. The words He spoke was not what she wanted to hear. She slowly walked away. Bobby stared after her.

She clearly respected Him, but probably wondered why He didn't know Lazarus was dead. In her mind, He was too late.

She turned back to Jesus, grief shadowing her face. "I know that he shall rise again in the resurrection at the last day."

Her comment triggered something in Jesus. This time when He spoke, his voice boomed—deeper, with power, like when Angel had spoken to Mary. "I am the resurrection and the life. He that believes in me, although he was dead, yet shall he live; and whoever lives and believes in me, shall never die. Do you believe me?" Jesus asked the woman.

"Yes, Lord, I believe that you are the Christ, the son of the living God which should come into the world."

He took her by the hand, and now his voice was soft. "Where have you laid him?"

"Lord, come and see."

They walked only a short distance when Jesus stopped in front of what seemed to be a small cave. "This is where he is buried," lamented the woman whose name was Martha.

Tears fell from the eyes of Jesus. Bobby couldn't believe it. A man with so much strength and so much power, and yet, He wept. It humbled Bobby to see how deeply Jesus loved others. Tears welled up in his eyes too, even though he never believed he could cry much about anything.

He tried to move closer to get a better look at the Man his mother prayed to and his pastor preached about every Sunday back home.

But Angel put a hand on his shoulder. "Stay here Bobby. Just watch."

Jesus spoke to two men in the crowd. "Take away the stone."

A murmur rippled through the crowd. Everywhere, Bobby heard the whispered question: "Take away the stone?"

Martha quickly spoke out, "But Lord, by now he is corrupt, for he has been dead four days."

131

When Jesus heard those words, judging by the fire in His eyes and the hardened tone in His voice, her statement appeared to be disappointing to Him. He looked her straight in the eyes and admonished her. "Did I not say to you, that if you would believe, you would see the glory of God?"

As he spoke, the two burly men Jesus spoke to rolled away the stone.

Jesus gathered His temperament, calmly kneeled down, and looked up to heaven and prayed. "Father, I thank You that You have heard me. For I know that You always hear me, but because of the people which stand here, I said it, that they would know that You have sent me."

He stood at the opening of the grave. The stone was now completely removed.

Bobby glanced at Angel. " He's going to—"

Angel cut him off with a single gesture to remain quiet. Bobby sighed. Angel's hushing and shushing was getting old. Bobby wanted to speak. He wanted to be heard. He wanted Jesus to hear him. He wanted to let Him know that he was different now— that he got the message.

Jesus stretched his hand toward the cave and shouted, "LAZARUS! COME FORTH!" His voice rumbled like thunder.

Some of the people covered their ears.

Some of the others moved away, seemingly in fear. But Bobby stood dumbfounded. Fear struck his heart too, not because he was worried about his life, but because he knew he was standing in the presence of God, Himself.

Something inside Bobby seemed to break at the very moment Jesus commanded Lazarus to come forth. His whole body contorted and seemed to be overcome with heat. It was a strange warmth, something he had never felt before. It was as though Jesus called him instead of Lazarus. He knew that within his own spirit, something was brand new—really new. The crowd stood in total silence, mouths hanging open, even though nothing had happened yet. And then he appeared—Lazarus, crawling out on his knees, struggling to come out of the cave and wrapped in burial clothes.

The people gasped. Some ran in fear, some fell to their knees praying to the God, and others shouted, "He alive! He's alive!" Still others began to repent and ask God for forgiveness. They screamed out their sins, asking God not to take their wicked lives. Bobby's body was rattled with runaway goosebumps that seemed to be searching for an escape.

Then Jesus looked at the people. "Loose him and let him go!"

Another strange sensation raced through Bobby.

He felt the weighty chains of selling dope fall heavy to the ground. He felt the ropes of disrespect and rebellion lose their stranglehold on him. He knew without a doubt he'd been set free. People around Lazarus shouted and danced and praised God. Even Bobby felt like shouting.

His world spun. He reeled in all of his senses that he could muster up and looked up into the sky, noticing the clouds were moving faster than normal. Everything around him seemed to be praising the Lord. Everything gave glory to God, and he wanted to give Him glory too. He wanted to shout and dance the way others did.

Then again, no one could see him, anyway. He'd probably look stupid praising God all by himself.

As if on cue, Angel tapped him on the shoulder. "What are you waiting for? Isn't that part of the problem today? People wait on others to express their joy about Christ. You have to learn to praise Him for yourself."

Bobby couldn't help the grin spreading across his face. He leaped and threw his hands in the air. He even shouted, "Thank you, God! Thank you, Jesus!"

Suddenly, in the midst of his adulation, a strange silence snuffed out the joy. An eerie darkness crept over the crowd. Bobby's elation turned to dread. The presence of something evil crept in.

134

When Bobby looked around, strangely no one was there. No Lazarus, no Angel—nothing. Was this the end of the dream? Was this the shadow of death he always heard about in church? He didn't want it to end this way—not now! He was just starting to understand things, just beginning to see why his mother always told him to put his trust in God.

A voice broke through the silence. "Bobby. Bobby!" It was a voice from the past—a sinister voice he'd heard before. It was LJ. "You can pay me now, or you can pay me later."

Bobby froze. This couldn't be happening. He saw the darkness and now he could even touch it. He looked around, and to his despair, it really was LJ. He stood there with two beautiful women on either side. They were finer than any of the women he'd seen in the club. Their clothes seemed to be made of gold, and silver. Their skirts hugged every curve, leaving nothing to the imagination. LJ was dressed in a black silk suit with diamond buttons. On his wrists were huge diamond and platinum bracelets, with a diamond-studded Rolex to match. They must have cost a fortune.

Bobby struggled to hold on to his senses. He gathered every scrap of courage and spoke to LJ.

"LJ, what are you doing here man?"

"Come with me man. God can't give you what I can give you. He can't do for you what I can do for you. I got fine women.

I got a pocket full of money, and a beautiful new Mercedes sitting outside—all for you, Bobby! Come on, go with me, man. I'm going to get you home dog!" Home, just the sound of that word was music to Bobby's ears.

The offer was tempting. Bobby looked around at the darkness and the strange silence. He looked at LJ and his women and his money. Could this be the way out? Maybe this *was* the way back to reality—the way back home.

"Come on, man. Trust me."

Bobby took two steps toward LJ.

Then another voice pierced the darkness, "Bobby, Bobby!" it was his mother.

He spun toward the sound of her voice. "Mama?" There she was, standing nearby in the darkness.

Then Robert appeared, surrounded by a misty cloud. He stood next to Mama.

Bobby frowned at his stepfather. "Robert?"

But Robert didn't respond. Still, Bobby could sense something was different about him. But what?

Bobby's mother moved closer to her lost son. She had Bobby's attention now like she never had before. He was ready to listen to whatever she had to say.

"Don't listen to him, baby. Jesus loves you. He loves you, Bobby. Can't nobody do you like Jesus!

He loves you. He loves you, Bobby. Choose Jesus!"

Bobby felt ripped in two different directions. His mother was saying the things he needed to hear. But LJ, along with his women and his money, were like a magnet pulling him closer to his addictions.

The illusions were back, and more real than ever. Bobby had already experienced a real taste of that lifestyle, and it was hard to let go. He and Mike had made so much money, so quickly. The money had a way of infecting a person. How could he ever go back to making a living the honest and right way?

Robert finally broke into Bobby's thoughts. "You can do it Bobby. I know you can, because I did it."

Bobby's eyebrows shot up. What did Robert mean? Had he turned over a new leaf? Did Robert give his life to the Lord? Was he truly going to be a father now?

Robert continued, "I never told you, but I was hooked on drugs for many years. I tried to push it behind me so I could appear to be righteous. I was too ashamed before my educated friends about my situation. It was a great mistake. I realize now I can help so many others by telling my story, rather than hiding it. Just say yes to Jesus, and He'll be there for you. I know, because He's there for me."

Bobby was confused now, his mind, in a thousand places. From old Tiger Stadium with his dad, to the back alleys of the eastside, to the glitz and glamour of LJ's club, and finally to the people who never even knew he was there. He struggled hard, trying to make the right decision. He knew he was in a spiritual tug-of-war. He could feel the fight between his spirit and his flesh. It was real. It was a fight everyone would have to battle somewhere in his or her life.

LJ's offer was extremely difficult to refuse. Bobby was frozen. He couldn't make a move. He wanted to do what was right, but he felt powerless against the strong illusions confronting him. Bobby was sure of one thing—that all his friends were facing the same demonic illusions, illusions that presented themselves every day of their young lives.

Suddenly, a hard, jolting smack on the back of Bobby's neck sent him reeling forward a step. *What the heck?* He turned around and looked straight into Angel's face.

"I see you're still trying to decide which way to go," Angel said. "You still trying to figure it out, huh, Bobby? You saw it firsthand! Didn't you see Him raise Lazarus from the dead? Didn't you see Him give sound to the deaf and sight to the blind? Didn't you feel his compassion for a sinner when He told people that whoever is without sin, let him cast the first stone?"

"Hey, Bobby!" LJ interrupted. "I ain't got all day!"

138

Angel moved directly into LJ's space and stood up to him, face-to-face. Angel looked like he had grown a foot, towering over LJ. His voice thundered. "You ain't got much time at all!"

Then he turned to Bobby. "Listen, Bobby, it only takes a little bit of faith, about the size of a mustard seed. Just stir it up and move toward the enemy and say, 'In the name of Jesus, get under my feet!'"

Angel's hands quickly pressed upon LJ's head in a vise grip, and under all the power that came through those hands, LJ fell straight to the ground like a giant oak tree. His women scurried away like frightened kittens.

Bobby looked at his mother and Robert, then pointed to LJ who was on the ground writhing in pain. "Mama, that's LJ!"

In unison, Angel, Mama, and Robert, looked toward heaven and pointed up. "But that's Jesus!"

"Put your foot on him, Bobby." Angel screamed as he kept LJ restrained.

LJ again was writhing in pain, "Ohhh. Ohhhh…"

Bobby hesitated.

Angel roared. "Get to steppin' boy!"

Bobby moved toward LJ, now with more courage than ever. With one swift movement, he put his foot on the back of LJ's neck. Then he lifted his hands high in total surrender to God.

A wonderful new source of strength poured through him—strength to turn away from everything that reeked of evil and from all the illusions that had surrounded him for so long.

He finally realized the truth. His fight wasn't with LJ, but with the devil himself. "Devil, you are under my feet! I'm serving Jesus! I'm gon' serve my Lord! God, I love you. Jesus, I love you. I give you my life!"

A proud smile stretched across Angel's face. "Go ahead son, get your praise on. Get it on now! God lives in the praises of His people. Your praise will strengthen you, and you'll need all the strength you can get for all I'm going to show you now."

C h a p t e r 8

The Conspiracy

Instantly, Bobby was clinging to the mast of a fishing boat. His sneakers skidded on a wet deck as he fought to keep his feet beneath him, as well as the men he saw that was always with Jesus. Where was his mother and Robert? Where was LJ? Where are the people who a moment ago was leaping and praising God? A storm was raging around them, and the disciples shouted to each other and their Master.

"Lord, save us!"

"We'll be destroyed!"

Bobby glared at Angel who appeared from nowhere. The heavenly guardian stood nearby on the storm-tossed ship, his hands folded in front of him and a slight smile gracing his lips.

"You've done it now, Angel. I don't see a way out of this one!"

Angel raised an eyebrow. "Really, Bobby? Have you forgotten everything we've been through on this journey—and so quickly?"

Bobby ducked under a spray of frigid water. Angel had a point. He'd taken Bobby along as they traveled with Jesus and the disciples. Bobby had seen countless people healed—shriveled hands renewed, the blind made to see, the lame made to walk. Even demons couldn't stand before Jesus. Bobby had lost track of how many wicked creatures he'd seen flee before the Savior.

His fingers nearly slipped from the wooden post. He dared a glance at the churning Sea of Galilee, and his stomach dropped into his feet. "I don't know, Angel. This feels different somehow. I can't swim!"

Angel chuckled, and Bobby had to fight the urge to smack him. "O ye of little faith."

Bobby heard the words in stereo, as Jesus said them to His disciples at the same time. The Master had finally been roused from his sleep below the deck. It was a welcomed sight to Bobby. Jesus lifted his hands toward the sea and shouted a command to the raging waters, "Peace! Be still!

Bobby's mouth fell open as the waves slowly stilled. The boat leveled out and Bobby's legs became solid beneath him again. The faces of the disciples mirrored Bobby's feelings.

What sort of man is this?

But, of course, Bobby knew the answer to that question. The Messiah. God Himself.

A grin spread across Bobby's face, it was too much for him. He turned to Angel. "When do we go home? I can't wait to tell everyone Jesus is real!

He's really real!"

But just as he said this, his thoughts switched to his brother, and for a moment, tears welled up in his eyes. Justin might not be alive. Bobby sunk back into depression, his faith instantly disappearing. He felt like the worst brother ever. As he looked at the men who followed Jesus and saw them repenting for their lack of faith, he too, felt like a loser.

As usual, Angel knew his thoughts.

"Bobby, you are no worse than anyone else. These men have walked with the Master and have eaten with Him, and yet, they still have sin. Your life is stained by the sin of the first man, Adam. A man is a sinner even before he has the first opportunity to sin. Something had to be done; someone had to pay for this."

But did that mean there was nothing Bobby could do?

Before Bobby could ask, Angel swept him up again. "There's something I want you to see."

Bobby's stomach twisted at the somber note in Angel's voice. He detected something dreadful in Angel's voice that made its way into his heart. It was like the feeling he felt when the time Angel told him he couldn't do anything about the children that Herod killed because it was already written in the logbook. "What is it?"

"You won't like it. It's not pretty, but you will understand it was necessary."

143

Bobby frowned. Why must his companion speak in riddles? But he thought it best not to question Angel about it. He'd learned that, at least.

As they traveled away from the boat, he held on to Angel like a young kid holding his mother in the middle of a thunderstorm during a dark night. It was an eternity to Bobby. When they came to a halt, they were in a place that looked like an ancient courtroom of some sort. White, marbled pillars, lined the front of the room. A half-sculpted bust of a man Bobby didn't recognize and a candelabra like one he saw in a church before, were the only décor in this cold-looking, sterile room. It was as though life didn't exist in this place.

There were those that looked like the Pharisees Bobby saw when he first met Jesus, except these men were dressed in clothes even more regal than the men he saw before.

One of the men stepped forward. He had the thickest beard Bobby had ever seen, and his voice rang with authority, as though *he* were the king of kings. "If all has gone well, we shall soon have this Jesus in our control."

Another said, "Yes, I hope you're right, Caiaphas. But I won't rest until he's cut off from the land of the living."

Still another Pharisee rushed into the room. "Caiaphas! The traitor has not failed us. We have

144

Jesus…and his followers have scattered like sheep whose shepherd has been smitten."

Caiaphas smiled. "Well done, where is he now?"

The Pharisee exuberantly signaled the soldiers by the door. "Bring Him in!"

Jesus was hauled into the room by a handful of soldiers. Bobby's heart sank. The face of the Man he had come to love was swollen with contusions. Blood poured profusely from his brow and His nose. His ragged clothes sagged from his body. His eyes were swollen, almost shut. His lips were cut and puffy. He was almost unrecognizable. Tears welled in Bobby's eyes. "How could this happen?" he murmured to himself. "Why did He let this happen?"

The soldiers thrust Jesus hard onto the stone floor. Bobby could hear Him moan.

"Jesus! We've been waiting for you. Isn't it a pity that your life of miracles should come to such a swift end? Maybe you have a miracle that will free you from this death?" Caiaphas sneered with a horrible look of hatred on his face. "Did you not say you are the light of the world? Well, things look pretty dark for you now, don't they?"

Jesus said nothing.

"Wasn't it you who bragged you were here on this earth before Abraham? Tell us, Jesus, just who are you? King of sinners, prince of the devils, giver of life,

145

or a dead dog?" Caiaphas leveled his gaze at the crumpled figure of a man on the floor.

Another Pharisee chimed in. "Jesus, did you say that Moses wrote of you? And did he write of us, Jesus, and this day? Did he? You told your people, 'Let not your hearts be troubled.' Tell us, Jesus. Anything troubling you now?"

Caiaphas then planted himself over Jesus, placing his foot on Him. "You said you were the strength of Israel, yet you don't have the strength to stand on your own two feet." He pushed him further into the floor, and then shouted to a soldier, "Stand him up!"

Jesus wobbled on his feet, barely able to stand. Bobby felt his heart breaking again. He wanted to help. If only he were alive in their world. He would crush them. If he had a gun, he'd blow them all away.

Angel sighed when he heard Bobby's thoughts. Bobby kept forgetting Angel could read his thoughts.

"Bobby, the weapons of our warfare are not carnal, they're not like the guns that shot your brother, or the spears the soldiers used to kill innocent children, but they *are* mighty when it comes to pulling down evil strongholds."

Bobby didn't know what Angel meant, but he guessed his gun fantasy was on the wrong track.

Caiaphas and the other Pharisees encircled Jesus.

146

Caiaphas spoke again. "Jesus, what is this damnable doctrine that you are spreading among the people, causing so much confusion and turning them against us

 Isn't it enough that we are troubled by these Romans? Isn't four hundred years of suffering enough?"

Jesus finally looked like He was going to speak, and Bobby felt a sense of relief. Even though he somewhat knew the story of Christ and how it would end, his mind never allowed him to embrace that reality. For him it was just church stuff.

Maybe now He will put an end to this mad questioning and torture. If He could calm a raging sea, surely, He could put an end to this craziness.

"I spoke openly to the world and in the synagogue where the Jews always come together," Jesus answered. "I have said nothing secretly. Ask those who heard me. They know what I said."

His remarks angered one of the soldiers who quickly moved in on Him and struck Him so hard, even Bobby recoiled. Jesus staggered a few feet away, trying his best to hold himself up.

The soldier looked at Jesus, "You dare speak to the High Priest so?" He struck Jesus again. This time Jesus fell painfully to the floor. Caiaphas approached him again. "Well? Speak, man!"

By this time, Jesus could hardly speak at all. His face was badly swollen and blood flowed from his mouth. Tears were falling from Bobby's eyes more than ever now. How could they beat a man who did nothing?

How could they beat a man who healed people? How could they beat a man who could calm an angry storm, saving lives? He did nothing to deserve this horrible treatment. Bobby's objections whirled in his mind.

Jesus spoke again through gritted teeth. "If I have spoken evil, then bear witness of the evil, but if well, why do you strike me?"

At that moment, a robust-looking man who wore what looked like some sort of breastplate of armor entered the room. A captain, perhaps? Bobby wasn't sure, but he could tell that this man was someone the others respected. Those who were enemies of Jesus stepped away from Him for the moment.

The soldier scowled. "What is it that you have summoned me for at this god-forsaken hour?

"Pilate, an enemy to Rome has been captured," Caiaphas responded boastfully.

"Here we are again. An enemy of Rome you say? Are not all you Jews enemies to Rome? What accusations are you bringing now…against this man?" Pilate questioned.

"This man is a malefactor," Caiaphas answered.

"A malefactor?"

148

"Yes, had it not been so, Pilate, we would not have troubled you this time of morning. We found this fellow perverting the nation, teaching throughout all Judea, starting from Galilee to this place, saying he himself is Christ. He calls himself a King!"

The anger behind the scowl on Pilate's face was in full force for all to see. "Is it always that we are troubled by your insurgents? These are very serious charges. Where are your witnesses for these accusations?"

Caiaphas shouted, "The people are my witnesses, Pilate! Yes, the people!"

Seemingly out of nowhere, throngs of people converged in the outer court. Their voices rang with anger and they hurled accusations and threats against Jesus.

Pilate waved his hand to quiet the people. Then he turned to Caiaphas. "You call these people your witnesses?"

"These are my witnesses, Pilate."

Pilate's frustration showed on his face in the beads of sweat dotting his forehead. "These people are nothing more than poor beggars! Look at them Caiaphas—it is no wonder they seek a messiah, as I have heard."

Caiaphas took a few bold steps toward Pilate. "Beggars, indeed, but they are my witnesses against this man."

149

Pilate slowly circled Jesus, warily eyeballing the man the whole country was talking about. Bobby's eyes drooped and he was glum as he looked at his helpless healer.

This is the man who can raise the dead. Why didn't He intervene for Himself now?

Pilate took his sword and lifted the face of Jesus ever so gently. He stooped low and looked directly at Him. He had heard so much about this man, and this was an opportunity to really see what He looked like. Jesus turned toward him and looked into Pilate's eyes, and the two men, worlds apart, stared for a moment as if suspended, frozen in time. Finally, Pilate came out of his trance.

"Behold how many things they witness against you." Jesus did not respond. Pilate snarled. "Don't you have anything to say?" But still, Jesus said nothing.

Pilate rose, disdain marring his features. He approached the Pharisees. "Take this man and judge Him according to your law."

Caiaphas wasted no time. "Pilate! You know yourself it is not lawful that we put any man to death."

"Oh, I see. You'd like for Rome to discharge your shame for you. How many times must I be exasperated because of your customs? You have become a bore to me!" Pilate then turned his attention to Jesus once more.

150

"Are you, or are you not the King of the Jews?"

Jesus was slowly moving, obviously in great pain, and lying in his own blood which now smeared the floor. But he managed a soft response. "Do you say this thing of yourself, or did others tell you about me?"

"Am I a Jew? The chief priests of your people have delivered you to me. Now you tell me: what evil have you done?"

Jesus was barely able to get His words out. "My kingdom is not of this world. If my kingdom were of this world, then would my servants fight that I would not be delivered into the hands of the Jews, but my kingdom is from another place."

"Are you a king, then?"

"It is you that say I am a king. To this end was I born, and for this cause came I into the world, that I should bear witness to the truth. Everyone that is of the truth will hear my voice."

At that very moment, Bobby knew Jesus was talking to him. It had to be, because he heard the voice of Jesus in his heart. Bobby heard the things Jesus said, and he believed Him.

Pilate retorted, "Truth? You dare to speak to me of truth? And what, what is truth?" Pilate sighed and shook his head. It seemed obvious he felt the issue was a religious one and not political. He turned to the people. "I find no fault in this man!"

151

The frenzied crowd roared louder than ever, hurling curses and other insults. It seemed certain a riot would break out at any moment. But Pilate simply raised his sword and shouted at the people. "Silence!"

The soldiers steadied themselves nearby, on high alert. The situation was getting out of hand. Pilate had to do something before things got any uglier.

"You have a custom," Pilate began.

But before he could finish, a woman burst into the room. It was obvious she was wealthy, judging by her clothes that were flourishing with gold, silver, and purple stitched patterns. Her eyes were wide with concern and the furrow in her deepened brow gave away the fright that possessed her. She grabbed Pilate's arm. "Pilate...you must listen to me!"

His red cheeks demonstrated embarrassment. "What are you doing here? This is no place for you."

"I must speak with you, Pilate!"

"No. Later. I have things I must attend to now."

She was Pilate's wife. She didn't release his arm. "It must be now. Have nothing to do with this just man, for I have suffered many things this day in a dream because of Him. Have nothing to do with Him! He's innocent, I tell you. He's innocent!"

Bobby's ears could hear Jesus struggling to breathe, heavier as each moment passed. What would Pilate do? How would he quiet the riotous crowd?

How would he control the bloodthirsty mob? How would he articulate to the people that he was the governor of Judea and not ruler of the Sanhedrin? He took his wife by the hand and ushered her from the room. "Be gone. This is no place for you. We'll talk later."

He slowly walked back toward the chief priests and scribes, maybe somewhat confused and perhaps growing a bit impatient with the whole situation. But all the while, he kept his gaze locked on Jesus.

Bobby interrupted the scene and pleaded with Angel. "Why can't we do something? There must be some other way! Jesus is dying! Please don't let him die. Please! Please!"

Angel never said a word. Bobby sat and stared at Jesus, defeated.

Am I going to die here, too?

He pulled his gaze away, turned to Angel, and tried again. "There has to be something I can do."

Angel shook his head. "It is already written. He is the Lamb slain before the foundation of the world."

Bobby struggled to understand.

Pilate interrupted Bobby's thoughts. "You have a custom, and by your custom it says that I should release one unto you at the Passover. Will you therefore that I release unto you the King of the Jews or Barabbas? Surely you would not select him over this man."

153

"Away with this man, Pilate! Free unto us Barabbas!" a woman from the crowd shouted.

With that, the crowd began to yell and scream again. Pilate's voice pierced through the commotion. "Barabbas is an insurrectionist and he is a murderer, but what evil has this man done?" He then turned back to Caiaphas. "What is it Caiaphas—why do you fear him? Perhaps he is stealing your popularity?"

Angry shouts roared from the crowd. "He's a crook! He's a blasphemer! He's a thief! He's a liar!"

"No! No! He's none of that!" shouted Bobby. But they couldn't hear him.

Pilate's command rose above the din. "SILENCE! You have well said, but what shall I do then with Jesus, who is called Christ?"

Caiaphas stood up and walked in front of Jesus. He stared at Him from head to toe, pointed at him, and with a voice dripping with cruelty, he said, "Crucify Him!"

Who is this man called Jesus?
Who does He think He is?
He would imply that He is a King
He can't deny that He said these things
Who is this man called Jesus?
Who does He think He is?
Where are the miracles you performed everywhere?
He's just an imposter
Look how He stands there

Who is this man called Jesus?
Who does He think He is?
Who is this man called Jesus?
Who does He think He is?
He said He walked on water
Raised up the dead
He said He is the Son of God
Why don't you crucify Him?
He said He healed the sick
On the Sabbath Day
Don't you know the law of the land?
Why don't you crucify Him?
You said that you healed the sick
And you raised the dead
Five thousand hungry souls you fed
Oh, but you're just a man
Born in all the land,
Now you're trying to make yourself into some kind of
God
If you raised up the dead
And made the lame man to take up his bed
Destroy this temple as we
Heard you say
And raise it up on the third day.
Don't you think it's very odd
For such a Man to act like God
Why don't you confess this thing
You're not a God, You're not a King
Bind Him up

He won't be still
Crucify Him on Golgotha's Hill!

———————————

The mob screamed and hurled their curses toward Jesus. They shouted, "Crucify Him! Crucify Him!"

There was complete chaos as people who had different opinions were at odds with each other, some nearly coming to blows. Pilate had indeed lost control of the pugnacious crowd. He pleaded with the crowd, as they became even more hostile. "Why? What evil has He done? I find no fault in this man."

One Pharisee departed from his pompous ways, shouting at Pilate, "We have a law, and by our law He should die like a dog! He made Himself the Son of God!"

Pilate faltered. His wife's words burned in his ears: *"Have nothing to do with this just man!"*

He kneeled before Jesus, almost as if he knew that Jesus was indeed a King. "Where are you from? Why don't you speak to me? Don't you know that I have the power to release you? And I, yes, I, have the power to crucify you?"

Bobby's heart ached, and a feeling of responsibility for what was happening to Jesus overwhelmed him. He knew he had abandoned Jesus long ago.

Every bag of weed he sold, every disrespectful word he uttered testified against him. Even the sagging, rebellious-looking pants he wore testified against him.

Jesus looked wearily at Pilate. "You could have no power at all except it were given to you from above. Therefore, he that delivered me into your hands has the greater sin."

In one last desperate attempt to get out of this situation, Pilate turned to face the mob. "You have brought this man unto me as one that perverted the people. And I, having examined Him before you, have found no fault in this man, as touching those things that you accuse Him. Nothing worthy of death is done unto Him. I will therefore chastise Him and release Him."

Caiaphas shouted out, "Pilate! If you let this man go, you are not a friend to Caesar. Any man who makes himself a king speaks against Caesar. Think, Pilate, think!"

"I have thought!! And I wash my hands, and I'm innocent of the blood of this just man. Make sure you see what I do!"

He began to wash his hands in a bowl of water and dry them with a towel.

A woman screamed from the crowd. "Let his blood be on us, and on our children!"

Pilate threw the towel into the crowd striking the woman. "It shall be done, even as you have required.

I shall release unto you Barabbas, who for sedition and murder was cast into prison, and Jesus, I will deliver unto your will, but first He must be scourged! Soldiers, have your way with Him!"

The ensuing beating was more than Bobby could bear to watch. Again, and again, they pummeled Jesus with blows so hard, that no ordinary man could have survived it. They surrounded Him like a pack of angry vicious wolves, fighting over their captured prey. They mocked Him and put a purple robe on Him, and bowed their knees saying, "Hail, Jesus, King of the Jews."

Bobby began emptying his heart of every devious thought, every sin he had ever committed, and every person he had not forgiven. It was a strange feeling. He was so distraught watching this awful beating, yet he felt a great sense of relief as he unloaded his sins. It felt like a heavy chain lifted off his neck.

One of the men fashioned a crown from thorns, the needles long and hard. He pressed it firmly on the brow of the Master. Blood spilled everywhere. It was difficult to watch, but Bobby knew it was something he had to see. He knew this was the reason he was here in this strange place. He had to see it. He had to experience it. It was the answer to his prayer.

Jesus collapsed to His knees. A half-crazed soldier used his whip to tear the flesh on the back of Jesus.

Again, and again, he struck Him with all the power his evil body contained.

Bobby moved away from Angel into a direct line with Jesus. He was face to face with his Savior. For a moment, he thought Jesus looked directly at him. He laid down right in front of Jesus, wanting to help, wanting to do something that could stop the carnage. Jesus looked so helpless, and yet there was a strength about Him that allowed Him to endure the pain. Bobby had a suspicion that everything they did to Jesus was for him.

His mind flashed back to Detroit. So many people were being hurt back home, addicted to the very illusions Bobby had been selling. Their lives were crumbling, and Bobby knew he was helping to shatter them. Drugs, sex, disrespectful to parents and teachers—all illusions causing the community to tear itself apart at the seams. It was what he did.

Robert's words stampeded back into his mind: "Have you ever read a book?" He knew Robert was right about how teenagers would rather fill their minds with garbage than read a book. After all, it's what Bobby did.

A loud crack from the soldier's whip refocused his thoughts back to the tragedy unfolding before him. Jesus' eyes fixed right on Bobby, piercing deep into his heart a new spirit. Although it was crushing Bobby to see Jesus bruised and dying, at that moment, it was like he and Jesus had become one.

Jesus stretched His hand toward Bobby. He moaned, as the pain was clearly shooting through every part of His body. His hands trembled, stained red with blood. Bobby reached toward Him. He could almost touch Him—just another few inches and he could help. Almost there and he could find some relief from his sins by helping.

But a lash from the soldier's whip cracked through the air. The whip struck Jesus and Bobby's hands. Bobby yanked his hand back. He could feel the astonishment settle over his own face.

"Angel, I felt the pain! I felt His pain!"

"No, Bobby. Not His pain, but your own. You see, every person will have to bear their own cross. The temptations you face in your life are nothing more than the pains of your sins. The whole world groans in pain until that great day when all of God's people shall rejoice at His coming."

His words did not make sense to Bobby. Bobby's heart broke at the sight of Jesus suffering. As blood poured from The Master's eyes, tears poured from Bobby's—uncontrollable tears, like when he was a kid after falling off his bike, badly scraping his knees.

"Why is He allowing them to do this?" Bobby asked Angel. "This makes no sense. This is the same man that stopped the storm and opened the eyes of the blind. This is the same man who raised a dead man from a stinking grave!"

But again, no answer came from Angel's lips.

A voice carried over the crowd. "It seems as though the bread of life has been broken! Let us see you walk on water now!"

One of the priest began spitting on Jesus. Caiaphas grinned as if he'd accomplished his mission. They were going in for the kill. Nothing would satisfy them until they saw Jesus hanging from a cross. The soldiers took hold of His limp body and dragged Him out, and all Bobby could do was watch. A piece of Bobby wanted to kill them, but he was quickly reminded of something he heard Jesus say. "Do good to them that despitefully use you and love your enemy."

Bobby glanced at Angel. "How can I love these evil men after what they've done?"

"And not just these men, but all men." Angel responded.

Can I love LJ, who shot my brother? Can I love Snake, who tried to kill me?

He watched them lead Jesus away to be crucified. His heart sank, and his hopes were dashed to bits.

———————————

They stripped Him and wounded Him
Pressed a crown of thorns upon Him
He suffered all night long,
To cover all our wrongs
He proved His love to all the world
Jesus, You loved me so

161

Oh Jesus, You Loved me so
You loved me so
You loved me so!

———————————

Bobby and Angel followed the soldiers through the streets. Jesus carried a huge, wooden crossbeam on his shoulders. Bobby knew Jesus wouldn't be able to carry it long, not after the beating he took. But he was determined to help Jesus in any way he could. He moved closer to the man from Nazareth. Maybe he could help Jesus carry the huge beam of wood. But another man was already there. Thank God somebody wanted to help. Thank God someone was brave enough to help Him.

Bobby still put his hands on the huge, wooden beam. He wasn't sure if it actually helped to relieve the load. Jesus looked at Bobby again, this time as though He were saying to him, "Don't worry about me. Save yourself from your generation."

With that, He walked onward toward His destiny, and Bobby toward his.

Chapter 9

Oh, What Love!

An unmerciful whip slammed into the flesh of Jesus, ripping it beyond recognition. He winced at the pain. Blood was everywhere. He had already fallen several times from exhaustion from trying to carry the heavy burden of that cross.

Another blow from the soldier's whip slashed across His back, leaving an unmistakable red welt. "Get up! Move!" The soldier spoke like a man who relished his job—who wanted everyone to know exactly how powerful he was.

Hasn't there been enough bloodshed? Hasn't there been enough pain and suffering? The thoughts flooded Bobby's mind, and it made him angry that so many people back home and around the world were so obsessed with violence and bloodshed.

He looked around, hoping to find Angel. Maybe he would have some answers. But Bobby's heavenly companion was nowhere to be found. Maybe he, too, couldn't bear to watch.

As Jesus marched on to His death, Bobby marched too, although now he was breathing heavily.

Even his body ached, and yet he carried nothing. His mind flashed with thoughts of his family. His father. He finally realized that he was angry with his father. His dad should have toughed it out. He should have been stronger and more determined, like Jesus.

The place where they marched was called Calvary; it had the shape of a skull. Bobby heard about it many times in church, especially at Easter, but he always missed the meaning or the purpose. Easter Sunday was the only time he went to church with his mother. He missed her so much. It wasn't until then that he realized how much he loved his mother. It was then that he wanted so badly to get back home so he could give his mother all the love she should have gotten from his father, and Robert.

When they finally got to Calvary, the heavy cross Jesus carried hit the ground with a thud. He was totally exhausted. His breathing was still heavy, and He was bleeding from head to toe. Bobby was surprised He was still alive.

Odd how Bobby's vision had seemed hazy at times while he and Angel traveled through this strange land. Yet now, the world around Bobby was sharp—clear as day.

He saw Mary. She was no longer the young teen who was in awe of Angel and the words he spoke to her. She was now a gracious and humble woman.

But still a mother. Bobby saw her face and the tracks of her tears from the dust of the land. Nonetheless, peace radiated from her—a peace Bobby couldn't quite understand. Another woman stood with her in support. She looked like the woman the Master told to go and sin no more. Some of His followers were there, and so were hundreds of other people, including many of the same folks who had previously condemned Him. Now they were crying.

One of the soldiers picked up a hammer and a few large spikes. Jesus stood like a lamb waiting to be slaughtered. He made no effort to stop the men from killing Him. He made no effort to plead His case. Did He want to be killed? Bobby struggled to make sense of it.

But then, it did make sense, in a way. He had a purpose bigger than the cross He carried—bigger than the pain He felt. He went to the cross willingly because it was His destiny.

The men grabbed Him, then picking Jesus up, they dropped Him heavily on the cross. He groaned in more pain.

He's God's Son, but He's still a man. The truth of it was hard to swallow. *He feels pain every bit as much as I would if I were on that cross.*

They stretched His arms wide so there was no slack in His body and then tied a rope just above His hands.

165

Bobby looked around again. Angel was still missing.

Why now, when I could really use someone to talk to? Bobby looked up at two other men already on their death crosses. He saw that they were ragged and badly beaten, and like Jesus, they were in a lot of pain, breathing heavily and waiting for the imminent arrival of death. As He sympathized with them, a heavy hammer came crashing down on the spikes that were carefully placed in the hands of the Man from Nazareth. The sound shattered Bobby's thoughts and sent chills all over him. Jesus screamed out in obvious pain.

———————————

Oh please don't let them crucify him
Oh please don't let them crucify him
Oh please don't let them crucify him
Oh please don't let them crucify him
They're going to scourge Me
They're going to mock My name
But for this cause into the world I came
They're going to beat Me
They're going to pierce My side
But in three days I'm gonna rise
If I don't die, on that old rugged cross
Then your souls will be lost
I got to give up My life for you
So you may know that My love is true
I gotta die...(song by Sharon Johnson)

———————————

Then more large nails were pounded through His feet, yet not breaking a bone. Again, He writhed and groaned in immense pain. He was King of kings and Lord of lords, and yet He couldn't escape the pain that saturated and overwhelmed his body. Bobby wanted to take His place, but he knew he didn't have the courage.

Two soldiers hoisted the cross into the air using ropes. The instrument of death dropped with a loud thud into a hole dug in the ground to keep it upright. Jesus groaned as the sudden jolt shocked His torn body. Bobby cried softly when he saw how uncomfortable Jesus was. Jesus tried to raise up to ease the pain in His hands, but as He did, He groaned from the unbearable pain in His feet. Even if His eyes were open, it would be hard to see because the blood flowed even more intensely from His brow. By now, others were crying, and Bobby was more willing to release his tears. He didn't want to be the only one crying, even though people couldn't see him.

Jesus' voice carried on the wind over the crowd of onlookers. "Father! Father! Forgive them, for they know not what they do." He shifted and winced. "I thirst."

Bobby was amazed. *Even in the face of death, He is still demonstrating His love. He could easily destroy everyone here with just a word from his lips.*

167

Just one word and all this would go away.

A nearby soldier dipped a stick with a cloth tied on the end of it into some vinegar and water, then lifted it up to the Man's mouth who had fed five thousand hungry souls. But Jesus spit it out immediately.

Why did He spit it out? Did it taste bad?

Bobby's mind flashed back to something he heard years ago in church, from his mother's pastor who was preaching on Easter Sunday. "It's because He wanted nothing that would ease His suffering."

Jesus was paying the price for the sins of the world. Because of Bobby, Jesus was dying. Because of Bobby, Jesus shed His blood. Because of Bobby, Jesus took the nails. Because of Bobby, they spit on Him and cursed Him. Because of Bobby, Jesus wouldn't come down from the cross—because He loved Bobby so! And not only for Bobby, but for the whole world.

Tears streamed down Bobby's face. Then he felt a warm hand on his shoulder, comforting him. It was Angel. He had returned. Relief filled Bobby for a moment, but still, he couldn't stop the tears from falling. He sobbed. "Angel, they're killing my Jesus.

"Your Jesus?"

"Yes, my Jesus. He's dying…He's dying for me!" Bobby could barely force the words out. His whole body trembled. Angel squeezed Bobby's shoulder.

"It's all right. Let it out. You've got a lot to cry for."

168

Bobby cried, "I heard Him say, Father, forgive them…"

Angel responded, "It is the message of the cross, forgiveness. It is why you are here—so you may learn to forgive others, and even yourself."

One of the men on a cross beside Jesus turned toward the Savior. "If thou be the Christ, save thyself and us."

The other condemned man gasped, and blood sprayed from his lips as he managed a reply. "Do you not fear God, seeing you are in the same condemnation? We are here because of our own action, but this man has done nothing wrong." He looked at Jesus. "Lord, remember me, when You come into Your kingdom."

Jesus turned His head slightly and said to the man, "Truly, I say unto you, today, you will be with Me in Paradise."

The words hit Bobby like a sledgehammer. He'd never seen anything like it. Jesus was dying, but He was still trying to offer life to the lost. No one in Bobby's 'hood would try to help someone who was a thug, or a murderer, or a prostitute, or even a homeless person. No one really cared about anybody else. People only looked out for themselves.

Suddenly, everything started changing. The sky grew darker, even in the midst of the day. In the distance, thunder rumbled, and Bobby saw flashes of lightning streaking across the horizon.

Jesus was barely able to lift His head toward heaven. His eyes bulged wide.

"Eloi, Eloi, lama sabacthani!"

Angel interpreted His words for Bobby. "My God, My God, why have you forsaken Me?"

Bobby trembled on the outside, but inside, peace spread through him. Peace like the kind Mary displayed. The words of the Man who calmed a raging storm were simple. "Father, into Your hands, I commit My spirit."

Bobby heard Him gasping for air. A soldier, holding his cloak against the strong wind said, "He saved others, but he can't save Himself."

Jesus struggled to speak His final three words. "It...is...finished." He took a final deep breath, then exhaled. His head dropped, His body stopped shaking, and He died. The only sign of life was the blood that still flowed from His wounds.

When the soldiers moved toward him, they thrust a sword into His side to make sure He was dead. Water and blood gushed out. Suddenly, the heavens opened up and a torrential rain poured down on all the people. The winds gusted like a tornado. All of nature seemed to recognize Him as the sky grew even darker. The frightened look on the soldier's faces told Bobby they knew something very profound was happening.

Bobby overheard one of the terrified soldiers say, "I have seen a hundred crucifixions, but never one like this. This Man was different from anyone we have ever put to death."

Angel had the same glow around him Bobby first saw around Jesus. Then the ground started moving in concert with the wind and the rain. People panicked. Some ran, others prayed with their heads to the ground.

As the rain continued to fall hard, a soldier moved slowly toward the cross and removed his helmet. He looked up at the lifeless body of Jesus. "Truly…this Man *is* the Son of God!"

The woman who was with Mary released Mary's hand and moved closer to the cross. She began to speak words Bobby had never heard, or at least didn't remember.

"But He was wounded for our transgressions. He was bruised for our iniquities; the chastisement of our peace was upon Him; and with His stripes we are healed."

When Bobby saw her move closer, he moved closer, too. He just wanted to touch Jesus, but instead, he could only touch His cross. It was as if some kind of barrier kept him from touching Jesus. The blood was still streaming down, and it flowed gently across Bobby's hand.

As the blood touched Bobby, he knew his heart had been healed. He knew he could forgive his father and Robert. He knew he could forgive LJ. Instantly, he knew he was forgiven from selling his drugs and his love for money and power. He knew he was healed from his deceptive ways. He knew he was delivered from lying, cheating, and everything evil his flesh desired. He knew that although he was delivered from all the illusions the world had created, illusions that hurt people and destroyed their futures, he knew he would never be perfect. At least not in this world. He also knew that his imperfect ways and weaknesses were perfectly forgiven by Jesus. He could see things for what they really were. He understood that the thief comes to steal, kill, and destroy. He finally got it—the enemy is the father of all lies, but Jesus offers the perfect answer. He wanted to thank Jesus, but all he could do was cry. He wanted to thank Him, but it was too late. He was gone now.

When Mary and the others who were closest to Jesus came to take His dead body down, Bobby was still at the cross. He desperately wanted to be like his Lord so he could carry the message of the cross to the world. He looked into his Master's face once more, and his heart caved in. He had never cried so much in all his life.

After the soldiers lowered the body of Jesus, the family rushed in. They lifted His limp body to wrap it. A couple of soldiers even pitched in. They, too, had tears in their eyes.

As they started to take Him away, Bobby couldn't hold back his emotions any longer. In the midst of a flood of tears, he screamed out, "Before you take Him away, I just want to say thank you Jesus!

Thank you Jesus! Thank you Lord!"

He didn't care if anyone heard him or not, he needed to hear himself. His tears flowed into his mouth. "I love you so much, Jesus. I need you! I'm sorry for my sins, I'm sorry for the things that I did! Thank You for giving Your back to those who hated you. Thank You for taking the nails in Your hands. Thank You...thank You." He turned his hat around, pulled up his sagging pants, lifted his hands in the air, and began to praise God.

———————

What wrong have you done?
Surely I knew of none
No one could really accuse you
For you gave hope to everyone
Look how they scorned you
And tore at your flesh
They compassed around you
Yet your wrath was at rest
I will never forget Calvary's cross
And all that was done here
For it is the place of my redemption
By the blood of Jesus
Whom I love so dear
So what kind of man is this
Who died for me and set me free

What kind of man is this
Who died for me and set me free
What kind of man is this
Who would leave His heavenly home
And come down
To give His life
Oh for a sacrifice
Just to save
To save a wretch like me
They beat my Jesus all night long
Until you saw every bone
But when He took His very last pain
He hung His head and died
For you and I
Oh what love the Man has for me
That He would give His life
Oh what love
He has for me
That He would give His life
That's love!

C h a p t e r 10

Home

Bobby fell to his knees. "I just want to serve You. I just want to be like You." He cried out again, "Please God, save me! Please God! Please! Please!"

Lightning streaked the blackened sky. But this time the lightning wasn't white. It flashed a rainbow of colors. Then clouds began swirling through the sky like years slipping by. Bobby felt like he was passing through what had to be the shadow of death, but he felt no fear.

If this is what God has for me, so be it. I'm ready.

Maybe Angel hadn't really stopped Snake's bullet. Maybe Bobby really was dead. None of it mattered to him now. Everything around him paled white. In his mind, he knew God had forgiven him. He was ecstatic. "Hallelujah! Hallelujah!" he shouted over and over. Even if he was dead, happiness filled him. He certainly didn't want to go to Hell, even though that's what he deserved.

No matter what, Bobby knew this wasn't the end.

He was born again. He felt a new life, a new beginning, almost like a butterfly bursting forth in new light from a chamber that held back all its glory and potential. He wondered if at any moment Angel would show up, take his hand, and lead him into God's presence.

Bobby closed his eyes and began to pray. "Our Father, Who art in heaven…" As he prayed, he felt a strange mist in the air. Droplets of water seem to baptize him into his new world. In his mind he was being cleansed from all that ailed him. Then he smelled a familiar scent. Granny's Mississippi Mud Pie.

He must be heaven! He was still thanking Jesus when he opened his eyes.

His mother stood over him, sprinkling water on his face. "Bobby? Wake up!"

Granny shuffled nearby, a plate in her hands. "See if he wants some pie, Emma."

"Bobby!" His mother slapped his cheek to rouse him. "Bobby, why are you on the floor like this? Robert! Robert, come here!"

Bobby's mind was swirling mist with nothing solid to grab onto.

Why am I on the floor?

Then his memory rushed back. Snake had come into the house with a gun. Angel, and more importantly, Jesus had intercepted the bullets meant for him.

176

He sat up and grinned.

"It's true everybody has an angel watching over them!" Mama looked at him like he was crazy.

Robert rushed in from the garage. "What is it?"

Mama's voice shook as she tried to explain. "I don't know. We came in and he was lying here."

Robert raised an eyebrow. "What's wrong with you, boy?"

Bobby's head throbbed, but his mother and Robert were a welcomed sight. He pushed himself up from the floor and wrapped his mama in a tight bear hug. "I'm home! I'm home! Mama, I love you. I love you so much." After a moment, he released her and turned to Robert. "Dad, I love you, too!!"

Robert staggered back a step, shock written all over his face. But then he reached forward and allowed Bobby to hug him, too. Bobby smiled. Maybe God had touched Robert's heart, as well.

"Mama!" Bobby suddenly broke free from Robert and turned back to his mama. "I wasn't here!"

"What do you mean you weren't here?" Mama frowned. "Bobby, what are you talking about?"

"I wasn't here, Mama. I was back in biblical times, two thousand years ago!"

Robert eyed him. "What do you mean biblical times, son?"

"I was back in the Bible days. Seriously!"

Robert's gaze settled on the floor, where the remains of Bobby's blunt still smoldered. He reached down and picked it up. "Wait a minute, Bobby, what is this?"

Shame swallowed Bobby's answer. He couldn't bring himself to admit it out loud. Not now.

Robert dropped his head. "Son, what were you thinking? This stuff is going to kill you!"

"I know, I know. But I swear to you, I was in biblical times."

Robert snorted. "If I smoked this stuff, I'd be back in biblical times, too!"

Bobby paced around the kitchen. How could he make them understand?

He took his mother by the hand. "You may think I'm on some kind of a high, but I'm not drunk. I'm on a Jesus high! I saw Jesus!"

Robert's mouth fell open. "You saw what?"

"I saw Jesus. He was real!" Bobby was so excited, the words tumbled from his mouth. "I almost touched Him, but He touched me first! There was a blind man, and Jesus touched him, and He said, 'Receive your sight,' and his eyes were opened! There was a deaf woman—she couldn't hear a thing, just like I was deaf and I couldn't hear anything you guys were saying to me. Mama, Jesus touched her ears and she began to hear. And Mama, He touched me, and now I can hear His voice, too!"

Bobby's excitement bubbled even higher.

"And then there was Lazarus. Lazarus was dead, and in the grave just as I was dead in my sin! I heard Him say 'Lazarus, come forth!' Mama, His voice sounded like thunder! Mama, Dad, I heard him shout to me, 'Bobby! Come up out of that mess!'"

He grabbed his mother by both her arms. "You gotta believe me. I'm alive, Mama! I'm really alive! I saw Jesus for the first time in my life. He's real. I tell you, He's real!" Bobby's tears had returned in full force. He wasn't sure what happened to him next, but he suddenly got a burst of joy, and a bright light glowed before him.

I'm in the presence of God!

Bobby jumped around the room, praising God, just like people did in church. "Hallelujah! Thank you, Jesus!" Then something hit him like a ton of bricks. All of a sudden, his joy was over. He stopped dead in his tracks.

Justin.

Bobby fell to his knees at his mother's feet, still crying, but this time in remorse. He was responsible for his brother being shot.

His heart weighed heavy in his chest. "Mama…Justin … I told him not to follow me. I'm sorry, Mama. I'm so sorry. Oh, God…"

Robert stooped down, grabbed Bobby by his arms, looked him straight in the eye and said, "Bobby, he's fine. He's in the hospital. We just left there. They had to do some minor surgery but he's ok.

The doctors couldn't understand the path of that bullet. It made no sense to them.

They say he's going to be just fine. He was actually talking before we left and believe it or not, he was more worried about you. He told me to tell you 'What's up?'

Bobby looked up. Could it be true? He couldn't believe it. He saw his brother's body lying lifeless in the club.

Robert squeezed Bobby's shoulder. "He's going to be all right, Bobby."

Hope rekindled in Bobby's heart. "You mean even today, in Detroit, Michigan, Jesus is *still* working miracles?"

"Yes!" Mama's eyes filled with tears. "Yes baby!"

"Oh my God!" Bobby sobbed, in awe of God again. "He's so amazing!" Bobby looked up at Robert. "Dad, I'm sorry for the things I did and the things I said. I'm sorry for the way I treated you."

Robert's jaw dropped again. But he recovered more quickly this time. Compassion filled his eyes. "I forgive you, son. And I hope you forgive me too, for not being the type of father I should have been—for not being there for you and Justin. That will never happen again." They hugged each other for what seemed like a

180

year. It seemed as if he was trying to make up for lost time.

Robert turned to Emma. "Honey, I'm asking for your forgiveness too, for the way I treated you. And by the way, I'm taking care of that gap, and you know what I mean. Never again."

Tears and hugs filled the kitchen. Even Granny got in on it.

She lifted her hands to heaven. "Thank you, Jesus. Thank you, Lord, for healing my family. Hallelujah!"

Thoughts of Jesus filled Bobby's mind again.

I want to be like Him. I want to love others the way Jesus loves.

He turned to his mama. "He died, Mama. He died and He never did anything wrong. Why did He have to die?"

She grinned at Bobby. "If you'd quit falling asleep in church on Easter, maybe you'd know the answer. It's funny. Even though the real message of the cross is preached every Easter and most Sundays, so many people still never get the message beyond the message."

"Mama, I got the message now—loud and clear. His message is love and forgiveness!" He looked at Robert. "By the way, you were right. Now I know what that cross means. Jesus proved His love for me and for the whole world. That's what I want to go tell Mike and

Tina. I want to tell them that they don't have to sell drugs or give in to what the world offers. I want to tell LJ that I forgive him for what he did to my brother. I never knew I could love Jesus so much. I wish I could have told Him, but now He's gone. I'm so sorry He had to die. I can't believe that He just died, and that's it."

Mama nudged Robert. "Tell him, Robert."

"Tell me what?" Bobby wondered aloud.

Robert paused for a moment. "Listen, son, He died for your sins, He died for mine, and He died for the sins of the whole world."

"I know, but then—just like that—He's gone. They killed him."

Robert smiled. "Boy, can't no grave hold that body down! He got up!" Robert's voice swelled, and he started sounding a lot like a preacher. "He died on a Friday, but early Sunday morning, He got up. He lives in you! He lives in me! He lives in anyone who will believe in Him. That's the message beyond the message!"

Finally, Bobby realized that when Jesus said, "It is finished," He spoke those words for the whole world. Bobby's old life had passed away and his new life had begun. He couldn't wait to get busy. There were so many people to see, so many people to tell his story to. He took off for the door.

Mama blocked his way. "Now where do you think you're going at this hour of the night?"

"I got to tell somebody what happened to me."

"Well, it can wait till morning."

A loud knock on the door interrupted their discussion.

"Emma, go get my gun," Robert instructed.

"No, Dad." Bobby stopped him. "We don't need a gun. Not this time." He turned to the door. "Come in!"

The door slid open. Bobby's stomach dropped and his heart thumped louder than ever. LJ's massive figure filled the doorway. Bobby scrambled to find his voice. "LJ, I'm gon' get you your money. All I need is some time."

Robert stepped in front of Bobby. "How much does the boy owe you? I'll take care of it first thing in the morning."

Then the most unlikely words Bobby ever heard came from LJ's mouth. "Forget the money. I couldn't get what went down at the club out of my mind. I was sitting there drinking and waiting for Snake. Then I just felt something. Something happened and I can't explain it."

His eyes looked watery. "Something made me come over here. I'm sorry for your brother, but I heard he's going to be all right." He shifted his weight and scratched the back of his neck. "Look, man, I'm giving up the club and I'm giving up the business. I can't explain it, but I can't do it anymore. It sounds crazy but that's how I feel."

Bobby didn't need LJ to explain it. "I know what happened to you. It's the same thing that happened to me. I don't know how, but somehow you met Jesus. That's how he affects people."

"Yeah…yeah…. well, anyway, I just wanted to say that to you, face-to-face, man-to-man." And with that, LJ headed back out the door.

Before he could leave, Robert stopped him. "Excuse me, but how did you find out about Justin so fast? We left the hospital not that long ago."

LJ turned back. "Some Latino guy came to the club. I never saw him before. Said his name was Angelo. There was something weird about him. Every once in a while, I thought I saw a strange glow around him."

Bobby looked up and grinned.

Angel, still doing his thing.

"Thanks a lot Father. Appreciate it!"

THE END

Jesus is the Lamb of God
He taketh away all the sins of the world
Jesus, He's the King of Kings
He's the Mighty God and the Prince of Peace
Jesus, He's the Lord of Lords
He's the Great I am and the Mighty Tower
Jesus, He lives!!
No grave can hold His body down
No man can take His life
He said destroy this temple
And in three days I'll raise it up
No grave can hold this body down
Why seek ye the living among the dead
Remember in Galilee He said
The son of man must be delivered
Into the hands of a sinful man
But on the third day I'm going to rise again

Let everything that has breath praise the Lord...Ps 150:6

To every person who took the time to read this book, I thank you. But more importantly, although the story of Bobby and his family may be fiction, the words and actions that are scriptural are truth. Everyone has a set of beliefs, here are mine based on words from the NIV Bible.

If you declare with your mouth that Jesus is Lord and believe in your heart that God raised Him from the dead, you will be saved. Romans 10:9

To God be the glory!

I'm so glad we got together
for just a few hours,
I hope I've made a difference in your life.
I am sure we'll meet someday beyond the
sweet horizon,
Until then...remember...we're friends.
—*TJ Hemphill*

To order a copy of the soundtrack for the stage version of Perilous Times please use the information in the front of the book.

Made in the USA
Columbia, SC
08 April 2023

15062145R00114